Blood Tender

Rachel Ingrams

D1424342

**Tindal
Street
Press**

First published in June 2008
by Tindal Street Press Ltd
217 The Custard Factory, Gibb Street, Birmingham, B9 4AA
www.tindalstreet.co.uk

A CIP catalogue reference for this book is available
from the British Library

ISBN: 978 0 9551 3849 2

Typeset by Country Setting, Kingsdown, Kent
Printed and bound in Great Britain by Clays Ltd, St Ives PLC

FSC
Mixed Sources
Product group from well-managed
forests and other controlled sources

Cert no. SGS - COC - 2061
www.fsc.org
© 1996 Forest Stewardship Council

For the real
Black-Eyed Man

Blood Tender

ONE

I

In my earliest memory of Jula, he is standing in Libost with his back against the wall. He is alone – you can tell by the wild, couldn't-care way he stands – and the funny thing is, he is laughing. It's the way I always think of him. Even on another Friday night, among the dope deals and the speed freaks and the blue skunk haze, among the junkies and their big eyes filled with burned-out dreams, Jula laughing. In this memory of mine he is standing there tipping his head back, tossing the black hair from his face and laughing out loud as if he has seen it all a thousand times before.

All around Jula people are dancing. They have these sad, skinny bodies and mad eyes; they're all high on dope and bad Catania speed. I know each dance, each face; it's always the same. And these dancers, they're like machines to me; they never stop, they just keep dancing, looking down at the floor. For it's a kind of nothing music they're dancing to again, some cheap Italian techno with a seedy beat – just a boom boom boom – and tonight the room is filled with blurred shapes and dark shadows, the club lights are flashing their green red green, and the strobes start to flicker and my head begins to swim, so I tell myself what I always tell myself whenever I walk through the door at Libost: that somewhere, beyond all this madness, life is good. Time is precious. Sleep is sweet.

In the chaos only Jula is still. Or at least, that's how I remember it – with him at the centre, the axis, the eye of it all; as if the room is spinning round him. And like I told you, he's laughing; he's laughing so wry because he's seen it all before, he's done the lot – the speed, the acid, the coke, maybe even the heroin – and to him it's just a joke now, this kind of life, just a lurid game. From the balcony a woman waves her arms and then shouts hysterically down. Two guys are on the floor fighting over a hit. But Jula isn't interested. He doesn't turn to look. In the memory only he is still. Even I am moving. I am moving towards him.

I can't help it. His is the only face in there which makes sense. Sometimes when I'm there I seek the outsiders, it's true: those lost-faced, blue-eyed souls; the ones who look a lot like me. But tonight I throw them half-smiles then I look away. I don't want to talk to tourists. I don't want their travel chat. I go right up to Jula, push sassy through the dancefloor crowd. Like I own the place, I arch my back against the cool stone wall and I laugh. And then I don't know what to say and all of a sudden I am nervous and I want to smoke, so in my best Italian I ask Jula for a light. When he doesn't understand I show him my cigarette; I smile into his face and I say Fire. Jula reaches deep into his pockets and the way he does it makes me feel he's got this endless stretch of time. I see that his hands and his hair and his clothes are all ragged and rough. I see his skin is olive-dark. And I ask him for his name and he says Jula and I don't know why but I ask him for his family name and he says Schigghiapeddi. It has a weird sound, a thick sound: 'Shkig-ya-ped'. I ask him what it means. Jula has a soft voice and I struggle to understand him, I have to put my ear close to the words and watch his mouth as they tumble out because the music is so loud in here and he is speaking in Sicilian dialect. For a foreigner that's hard, but in the end I get it: Jula is telling me that his name means something strange, something like little cries of skin, little skin squeals. I laugh in disbelief and look up at Jula Schigghiapeddi and into his eyes and in the flashing disco darkness I see that they are almost black: black and shining, black and ragged, black and wild, and secretly I name him to myself Jula of the Little Skin Squeals, Jula of the Little Hurts, Black-Eyed Jula of the Little Wounds. And for a moment I do nothing but whisper that name down into my heart and I stare.

2

The night I arrived in Sicily there were riots in the streets. It had been coming for weeks, the taxi driver said: violence, just hanging there in the air. It was bound to happen, he said, any fool could have predicted it. Why, it was so hot this year, Lamorte was on his way in – and men, after all, were men. Maybe he was right. Maybe it was unavoidable. I couldn't stand heat like that. It was the kind of thing that made me sick in the head.

I remember the way it hit me when I stepped from the plane: hot air shimmering in waves over the tarmac, dust rising in clouds and moving like water over the ground. The runway was lined with palm trees; the sky was a bloody gold. It was different from anything I had known.

Walking through customs and out past a string of airport shops I saw local newspapers on display. One front page showed flames, black smoke billowing out from a window: faces, fists, eyes gleaming. Then the tabloids, selling their bigger news – snaps of Gianmarco Lamorte cruising the last days of his campaign. Lamorte looked smooth, set to win. The headlines said so too, and were already celebrating: *Viva Lamorte! Viva l'Italia!*

I bought a paper and hailed a taxi. The driver reached over and swung open the door. I looked in at him; he had on a white shirt and mother-of-pearl cufflinks. He was trying to push the cap off a tub of painkillers with his thumb.

I climbed in, lowering my head.

'Where you going?'

'Monte Tesoro. Via Rosa.'

'Monte Tesoro?'

The cap flipped in the air and landed on the guy's knee. He tipped the tub up to his mouth, swallowing a couple of pills.

'We'll take the backstreets,' he said. 'I don't want trouble.'

Driving the small roads, we passed cars burned out, their windscreens smashed, streets strewn with shattered glass. All the trash cans were upturned, garbage spewing on to the ground. I saw a tree on fire. Big flags rolled down from windows with Italian colours blazing – and banners stretching from lamppost to lamppost proclaimed the same as the papers: *Viva Lamorte! Viva l'Italia!*

'What's going on?' I asked the guy.

'It's Feo, creeping around the corner! You can bet on one thing, *signorina*: this is not the end!'

He ran his fingers through his hair.

'Who's Feo?'

'Ha! He's a Nazi is what he is. He hides it from the media – *che camaleonte!* – but you should see him at the rallies, *signorina*: all hush-hush in the backrooms and bars! He's doing deals with Lamorte – big deals! I had this friend, you know, he filmed him once in secret. With a little camera – a camera, in a bag!'

We stopped at traffic lights. He lit a cigarette and handed me the pack.

'I couldn't watch that footage,' he said. 'I had to leave the room.'

'Where are you from?' I asked as we reached a dual carriageway and the car picked up speed.

'*Napoli*. You?'

'I'm English.'

'English?'

Suddenly he seemed to forget Feo, the secret filming, the fires and flags. He grinned and patted the steering wheel as if he were a child.

'From Great Britain!'

I turned away from him.

'It's not so great,' I said.

He glanced at me and stayed silent. In the shadows I shuffled and blushed. It was only as we drove further away from the bright airport lights – as I turned to watch the planes curve up into the evening sky – that he whispered: 'English? British? No problem. Nothing wrong.'

It was dark by the time we reached my accommodation. The meter flashed a price in lire, a great big number. It was thousands of something, meaningless to me. I handed the guy his money and stepped into the street with my case.

'Thanks.'

He put his hand flat over his heart and gave me his business card. It had a picture of a taxi on it and his name in black capitals: BUFALINO ARNALDO.

'In case you need a ride again,' he said. 'I don't charge any tourist price.'

'Do others?'

He looked at me, incredulous. Then he leaned across the passenger seat to insist:

'Be careful, little British. Every man here is a thief.'

3

The tenement gave me the creeps. It was right out on Catania's southern edge, in Monte Tesoro – close to the *zona industriale*. Monte Tesoro was a rough quarter, known for its junkie crowd, its chemical plant – and Mickeys. Mickeys was where I worked. It was just a strip club. It was no big deal. You could see it from the motorway; its sign was a long, pink kicking leg with the club name flashing across it in blue neon like a garter:

MICKEYS MICKEYS
MICKEYS MICKEYS

And on the shoe-tip were the words:

OPEN 24 HOURS

The junkies were no big deal either. At least, they were nothing new to me. But the works – a cluster of old brick buildings down by the river – the works were a death-house, and the only hope of a real job for miles. As tall and thin as devils, you could see the factory chimneys from anywhere in Monte Tesoro, see their smoke blasting up, their chemical flames. I couldn't stand on my balcony for more than a minute without coughing. And I couldn't bear the smell. Whenever people talked about Monte Tesoro they always joked about the stink. They said if you came from there you would never find a lover. No one had anything good to say about the place. No one wanted to live there.

The block of flats stood on its own by a wood. The trees were silver birches. The wood was dying. From a distance you couldn't tell; it was just like any of the birch woods back in England – so slender, with all that grace; those long, shining trunks reaching up for the sky. But the first time I got close I knew something was wrong. The grass was bright yellow; some of the tree branches were rotten. They were falling off; they were shrivelling. They had no leaves.

The locals said it was normal; that all city trees die. And maybe I would have started to believe it too if I had stayed there longer – you know, the way you do. But I'm not dumb. It was obvious to me what was happening. The wood was being poisoned. It was too close to the factory to survive.

To reach the tenement from the road you crossed a piece of wasteland; the grass there was the same lime yellow. It had been a play park but now it was a dumping ground; the swings were rusty and the roundabout was bust. I used to sit on it sometimes, try to pretend I was a kid again – but I could never get it to turn. Someone had fucked it up by jamming a load of bricks under the base.

Nobody used the park now but the junkies. They would sit on the swings and shoot up. I liked to watch them from my window, see them traipse around like ghosts as the sun was sinking – talking, laughing, tripping out in the dusk. Sometimes I'd find their dirty works, their syringes scattered amongst the stones. I used to count how many I could spot on my way to work. I like to count. It makes sense of things. When I feel alone, I like to count. One, two, three, four: steadying me, reminding me who I am.

Stumbling across the rubble with my case I heard more riots, police sirens whooping in the air. The shapes of wrangling trees surrounded me – and it was hot, so hot, with the smell seeping out from the chimney stacks. I covered my mouth with my jacket collar. I wanted to go home. I thought about leaving – getting back on a plane. But it was too late. I had a job set up. Pretty soon I would be sequinned, topless, raising my arms above my head; moving slowly from side to side on a club stage for men with money and smiles. People call me a dancer and I guess that's what I am – if a dancer is someone who can make her body answer to music and nothing more. Who was I kidding? What had I to go home to? There was nothing for me in England except trouble and debt. When I looked back over my shoulder, Arnaldo's taxi had gone. Squinting into the distance, I could just make out the traces of his tail lights as they faded into the night.

4

'You're very late.'

The girl peering through the crack in the apartment door had bleached blond hair and flitting eyes. She had one of those broken-heart lockets dangling around her neck.

'We thought you weren't coming.'

She opened the door wide and I smelled bleach. Cheap perfume, polish. Cooking meat.

'There were riots all over town,' I replied. 'We had to take a longer route.'

She smiled, but I didn't like the way she did it. It made me think of a snake. It was too much tight lips and lipstick; it was too much lies. It was the kind of smile that never reaches the eyes – eyes which anyway don't look at you straight.

'You must be Carmela,' I said.

'It's Carme, actually.'

Her voice was nasal; her words came out in a kind of whinny.

'I'm Marlena,' I told her. 'Marlena Lupone.'

She flared her nostrils and stuck out her chest as my name rang like a bell in the dark.

I hate those broken-heart lockets. Like you can belong to someone else. Carme shook her hair and turned away. She shouted through to a room behind her that *l'inglese* had arrived. I craned my neck over her shoulder, saw a TV flashing, a bird in a cage. I heard surround-sound voices; I glimpsed an armchair and the back of a guy's head.

The bird squawked.

'*Finalmente*,' said the head, without turning.

'My man,' Carme said.

Like the landlady of some hideous provincial guest house she took me from room to room, letting her hand fall on to brass ornaments and pot figurines as we passed them by. The meat smell coming from the kitchen grew heavier.

'I suppose you wish to eat?' she asked.

'Not really. No.'

She huffed out a sigh.

'So, you've done this kind of work before?'

'Uh-huh.'

'Mickey says you're half-Italian, is that right?'

'I was born in Venice, if you want to know. My mother came from Burano. But I had an English father.'

'Well, Mickey's English too,' she said. 'Maybe that's why he drags in strangers. English, like your *papà*. You can talk to him.'

I watched her as she brushed a little bird feather from her skirt.

'What's he like?' I asked.

'Mickey?' She looked me up and down. 'He likes his girls clean and tidy. He's very particular. Like me, in fact: he's someone who knows what they want.'

Carme shook the hair from her shoulders again and laughed dully. I wanted to laugh too. I didn't believe what she said. She seemed like she had never known what she wanted. I had met girls like that before. I decided she was like them. I decided she was dumb. I glanced about me and shivered. I gazed down at the waxed floors.

'He likes a clean house,' Carme said.

'Who? Mickey?'

'No.' She tutted. 'My man, of course. Blasto.'

I didn't understand. The name sounded like a kind of washing powder or something.

'*Blasto?*' I said.

But Carme didn't reply. She just pulled at her locket, smoothed down her skirt and smiled the snake smile once more.

As she took me to my room I saw there were mirrors everywhere. I can't stand mirrors. I don't like what they do. Of course I have one for work; I keep it in my pocket. I flip it open and check my make-up sometimes when no one is around. But to look into one for pleasure – smile for the glass, pose: I can't do that. It doesn't make me feel good.

My body is thin and pale. Sometimes my ribs push up at my skin. If you look at me long enough – close, naked, and in the light – you can see needle scars dotting my arms; my legs too, my hands and my feet. Even in darkness, my body won't lie. With your fingertips flat in the space between my breasts you can feel three hard, raised bumps. They are cigarette burns. They were once blood-purple. They sit like jacket buttons in the centre of my chest.

I like my eyes the best. They are blue, flecked with yellow. They don't change or fade. They don't scar. And how I like to see them is soft, distorted, in the eyes of someone else; my face broadened and laughing, my smile answering back and back.

'Did you see Feo on your way here?' Carme asked.

'The politician guy?'

'He came to speak tonight in the *piazza*! Did you see the crowds? I think we may have won!'

She pulled a ribbon from her shirt pocket and hung it along a mirror frame. It was striped in Italian colours: red, white and green.

'We?' I asked.

'*Viva l'Italia!*'

'You support them?'

'Well, yes . . .' She started to toy with the ribbon-end and fray it. 'Yes,' she repeated nervously. 'I do.'

'Listen, Carme,' I said. 'I'm not political. I saw nothing tonight. I've come here to strip, just like you do. To dance at tables for men.'

Carme coiled her false yellow kinks round her fingers, her eyes darting towards me and then away like flies.

'Well then, you'll get on at Mickeys fine,' she retorted. 'As for me, I'm not a stripper. That's not what I'm trained to do. I'm a kissogram. I'm not planning on staying.'

I laughed out loud. 'Who is?'

Carme stopped trying to talk to me after that. She opened the door to the back room. There was a table in there and a single bed.

'These are yours,' she told me, dangling two silver keys in front of my face. 'Don't lose them. The last girl did. There's one for the main door, one for inside.'

I reached out and took the keys from her.

'*Buonanotte*,' she said, twisting on her heels.

I put down my case and walked over to the window. With my face pressed up close to the glass I could see the factory and the wood. The main chimney loomed – it was far higher than our block. It was brick-built and smoke-stained; it had iron ladders running up it and a light flashing from its top. I counted. Every seventh second the room turned crimson.

I lay down on the bed, heard the guy Blasto laughing flatly along the hall. Then Carme tittering in echo like a jester, a fool. I wondered briefly about them – what their love was like, what Blasto was doing there. But I didn't think for long. I was tired. Too tired to lower the blinds or undress. Still in my coat and shoes, with my new keys in my hand, I closed my eyes and slept in the changing dark.

5

Libost was the place to be when I was in Catania. I could never understand why. The owner, Lukáš, he was all right – most of the Czech crew living in Catania then were all right – but his club, at least by the time I saw it, was a loveless, box-shaped place. It was full of junkies.

In Czech, *'Libost'* is an old word meaning 'pleasure'. I used to laugh at that – because of the junkies, because there were so many of them. Because they were all so worn down; so tangled up and sad. Lukáš tried, but he couldn't get rid of them. He used to kick them out when he found them mainlining on the balcony but the next time they showed up he just took them back. Then he used to welcome them in, take them to his favourite corner of the bar and get the girls to bring them free *madaleine* and tea.

'People fall on hard times,' he would say if I asked him why he did that. Lukáš: sometimes I miss him. He was so young and mild, with his shy, gap-toothed smile, his low-looking eyes, a burst of sandy curls around his face.

'Next time round it could be me with the spike in my arm,' he would laugh. 'It could be you!'

'Don't say it, Lukáš!' I would cry. 'Don't say it!'

Repeating my words until he mumbled soft – almost inaudible – his There But For The Grace Of God.

*

I had been going to the club a while when I met Jula. I used to go down most nights after Mickeys – to get away from Monte Tesoro and out of Carme's flat. On that first night talking with him I didn't believe some of the things he said.

'You're inventing stuff!' I laughed, but he only shook his head.

For the tales he told were of another world – they were of Etna. *Mongibello*, he said they called it – Beautiful Mountain, where a violet could grow on a river of lava, where the air smelled of honey and oranges, where there were eagles and vipers and wolves. There were cracks you could fall down and never come out of again on the Etna roads, he said – and deadly tunnels and big stinking craters. Jula reeled off names: Rinazzo, Fornazzo, Mascali. He said the volcano's eruptions had wiped out whole towns. His stories made me forget myself – what was happening in Catania, forget Blasto and Carme, the dancers and the drugs. I listened to Jula, as he fell into that low, raw guttural – so coarse and tender, such a mixed-up sound.

We didn't stay inside Libost for long. It was too loud.

'I can't hear you!' I kept saying. Or, if he strayed too far into dialect: 'I don't understand.'

'Come on,' he said eventually. 'We'll go out the back.'

He led me through the bar, where a large-breasted girl was tipping vodka into brass optics. She gave me a sultry wink, then she nodded at Jula and pursed her lips. Jula asked her for a few bottles of beer. He took me through a disused kitchen and along a corridor – and suddenly we were out in the open air, standing side by side in a yard filled with pallets and crates and silver barrels all stacked against one wall.

'You know people here?' I asked.

'I guess. I know Lukáš.'

He stepped further into the night.

'I always come out the back,' he said. 'It's my little paradise.'

The club music was much quieter now, deep and muffled like a pulse. Over the wall the sky hung close. It was filled with clouds, dull orange with electric light – and starless. I sat down on a crate.

'You a student?' he asked.

'No. I work out in Monte Tesoro. At a place called Mickeys.'

'The strip joint?'

'You know it?'

Jula handed me a beer.

'My little sister used to work there, until she went totally off the rails. I had a girlfriend there too once, but that's going back. I was just a kid then. Jesus, time goes so quick. I used to go out to Mickeys every Saturday night.'

The thought of Jula watching women strip sent a prickle down my back.

'What was her name?' I asked.

'The girl I had? Her name was Sonia.'

'Oh,' I replied, relief coursing through me. 'I don't know anyone called Sonia.'

'No,' he said, smiling. 'She quit. She got sick of Mickey.'

He started to laugh and then added as an afterthought: 'So she left the place. Then she got sick of me.'

I couldn't think how any girl could get sick of Jula. I breathed in tight and sipped my weak beer. It seemed like we had been sitting there forever when on the other side of the wall a car pulled up. The brakes screamed; we heard tyres burn against the kerb. Someone got out and slammed the door – then they ran along the street towards the club. Jula stood up and turned his ear to male voices in the distance.

'I think someone's looking for me,' he said.

'You want to go back inside?'

'No need. They know where I am.'

Over the wall, the car engine was still running. The window was open; the radio was on. Out poured the blues, Billie Holliday slurring 'I Cover the Waterfront'.

'What is it about, this song?' Jula asked. Then he added, answering himself: 'It must be love.'

We smoked some grass in a pipe Jula had. We laughed at stupid things. Then I asked more about his name: Schigghiapeddi. I knew it was something special. It went back centuries, Jula said. It belonged to a family of fruit farmers living on the volcano – on Etna's foothills, before the black scree and dust begin; up north, past Taormina. Even now, everyone knew the Schigghiapeddi groves: they were huge – and many; they dipped and grooved around Etna's base, following the contours of the rock. From certain points in Taormina – above the open-air theatre or balancing like a high-wire act on the bright, geranium-covered walls of the Hotel Grand – you could see them if you knew where to look, for they were vivid green, lush; far greener than the rest. If you wanted the best fruit in the north-east, you went to Giosetta Schigghiapeddi. Lemons, oranges, limes, sweet mandarins: Jula's mother had them all.

Taormina is this tourist town up the Sicilian coast. It's famous for some writer or other, don't ask me who. It's beautiful all right, everyone says it's beautiful; and if I ever tell anyone I lived not far from there they chime, 'How pretty, how sublime!' But Taormina, no: that's not my idea of heaven. It was always packed out with beach-freaks and fat-faced tourists walking crocodile-style along the cobblestones.

'It used to be different,' Jula said. 'Even ten years ago, no one really wanted tourists here. No one cared about the money; no one wanted them to come. Now we've all sold out, bought into the game. There's hardly anyone I know here who doesn't own a bar or a boat or a couple of rooms out on the front.'

'Or a strip joint,' I added, and we laughed at that. And Jula took my hand and squeezed it – playful, strong – and when I looked up at the sky I saw it was changing. There was a breeze now; the clouds were shifting. I could just make out Orion's belt – and the North Star, peeping through.

Standing there in the yard, Jula told me he was half-Romany. That his blood name was Hanuvat, his real father back in Romania.

'So why did she call you that skin squeals name?' I asked, as he opened another bottle with a knife.

'My mother? You'll see what it's like around here. She did it to avoid disgrace.'

'But Schigghiapeddi – your stepfather? He must have known, didn't he?'

'For sure. Some hag from the fish market went and told him. Even if she hadn't he would have known it. Can anyone really hide a love affair?'

He looked up at me, resigned, amused.

'And you know what? When my mother came back home that night he went for her with an axe! He was an animal, Jesus, and he was drunk that day – everyone says he was always drunk – and so he picked it up, the axe from the woodshed, he took it and he ran with it, screaming and all sorts and calling her Judas. Then he had a heart attack. *Ha avuto un infarto!* He dropped down in front of her. Just like that.'

'He's dead?'

'Yeah.'

Jula took a final drag on his cigarette and flicked the butt on to the ground.

'You get what you deserve,' he said. 'Sometimes you get more.'

Suddenly we heard footsteps again. Someone was running back to the car outside. Jula lifted a finger to his lips.

'Lukáš?' he shouted. 'Is that you?'

A young man's voice sounded back over the wall.

'It's your sister, man. It's Analisa. Get in the car, man. She's done it again!'

'Shit. I'm coming. Ana, shit. Hang on. I'm coming. Help me down.'

Jula looked at me as he picked up his cigarettes and pipe from the ground.

'See you around,' he said. 'I've got to go.'

He climbed up the beer barrels stacked against the wall. I watched him as he hauled himself up to the top and jumped into the street below. He was maybe six feet tall, a little heavy – yet he was quick and strong. I watched as he disappeared. I heard his voice, talking to the others. Then the car door slammed again. They pulled away sharp.

I sat there on the bottle crate for a long time. I drank one of the beers Jula had left behind. I had another, and another, until I started to feel drunk. I didn't want to go back inside Libost. I didn't want to go back through the bar or see the girl who had pouted and smiled. So I climbed up the barrels like Jula had done, grazing my arms as I pulled myself up on to the wall. There I saw an empty street; beyond that, Catania, stretched out and sleeping. I smoked my last cigarette and swung my legs, wished somehow I had said something; asked him for a number, shouted out. But shouting out: that isn't right. My blood tells me what to do. My bones talk. And they told me to hold tight as he left – to freeze, be quiet, wait. So I stayed on the wall-top with a tipsy smile and counted the regulars as they stumbled from the club into the night – still looking to the ground, still moving to a music they could no longer hear. Then I jumped from the wall and slunk off with my arms dirt-smeared and stinging, began the two-hour walk back home to Monte Tesoro, my head calm and confident, my heart swelling like an ocean with the promise of a man.

6

Carme had strange views. Fixed views. I was certain they weren't her own. I mean, I never knew her dreams, never came up close – but I couldn't believe she was really into all that fascist stuff. All that *Viva l'Italia* crap. Still, right from the start, from me standing in her hallway with my suitcase in the damp and the dark, the smell of broiling meat wafting round us like a sickness, I could feel her politics between us. I don't have time for that kind of thing. It's just a waste.

Sure, sometimes when she was away from the flat, sometimes at Mickeys when she had no one to answer to – no one, that is, except Mickey himself and he was hardly ever there – I saw her act begin to slide. Some nights in the booths I would watch her talking with a man in ways she never talked at home. She could be brave, she could be brassy; she could shake her hair back from her face and really laugh. But mostly Carme was jumpy, unsure, her small lips twitching, her mouth poised for some inane attack.

I almost told her, once – told her how I liked her so much better without her mask. It was on my first day at Mickeys, after the shift had ended. We were up in the dressing room. It was about four in the afternoon and I was drunk; I had been drinking whisky with a man from the States – some tourist guy from Maine. Carme and I were standing at the sinks, both of us tired, half-naked, navy-black smudged around our eyes and the lipstick on our mouths worn to pink. She was looking down at her body. She was taking the silver tassels from her breasts.

'Hey,' I said. 'Carmela.'

I put a flat hand between her shoulder blades, felt them stir under my palm like stunted wings – and suddenly I felt sober. I lifted my head up to face her and opened my eyes wide. I looked right at Carme and I saw her, I really saw her there – and for a second, you know, I think she might have seen me too, because her spine straightened slightly under my touch and she stood up tall; her lips parted and she uttered my name like a plea: '*Marlena!*'

It was the only time I ever felt close to her. It was the only time things ever felt right. Standing there then under the striplight in the silence and stale air – for a moment equal, truthful with each other; free. But it didn't last. She bristled and moved away from me; she reached for her shirt, saying: 'I have to go. Have you seen my watch? Blasto's waiting for me. There's a rally in town.'

'You don't seriously go for that bullshit, do you?'

'It's not bullshit, Marlena. You're drunk. Blasto says . . .'

'Yeah, yeah,' I laughed. 'Blasto, Blasto. So what if he's waiting? What kind of a name is that anyway?'

She stared at me, her mouth quivering.

'I'm smarter than you think!'

'Oh?'

She didn't answer. The moment was gone. No, I could never have got near to Carme, never have been her friend. Not the way things were. Not with her man at her side.

I don't know where Blasto lived, but he never went home. He was always hanging around the flat. He was a leech. He was forever taking food from the fridge and asking

Carme for money. He was always talking on the phone and shouting into it. When I asked him what he did, he just said he had business in Catania.

'It's the future,' he would say.

He let me guess the rest. He had a few cronies – young, gloomy faces; faces that were always changing. Kids came and went, picking up flyers for Antonio Feo to distribute around town. They didn't get any money for it; Blasto had roped them in somehow. Only a handful of them stuck around. They hang in my memory.

There was Vito Cornelli, with his sickle-shaped scar, his top lip always trembling under it like some teenage Elvis. His girlfriend had been killed a few months before we met, hurled through the windscreen of Vito's car. He had escaped; he just unhooked his seatbelt and walked to where she lay. He used to talk about it for hours. It went round and round in his brain, he said. I tried to talk back to him, but he had this way of looking at me when I opened my mouth, like he couldn't hear what I was saying, like he didn't understand. His scar was crossed with six pink stitchmarks. It shortened when he talked.

'I murdered her!' he used to moan. '*Mio Dio, l' ho ammazzata!*'

There was Laura, too. Blasto was fucking her on the sly. She couldn't have been more than sixteen. She was timid and bland. Whenever she arrived Blasto would shuffle her out on to the landing, locking the door from the outside, waiting for the flick of the automatic light – and I would hear them through my wall, hear her protesting: 'Not here, please, Blasto, no!' Then her words would stop and the noises begin. Who knows if Carme knew. She never said.

Then there was Goffo. Out of all of the hangers-on, he was the one I knew the best. Poor Goffo: he was geeky and pock-marked and built like an ox. He was the son of a tailor, his father's apprentice. It was funny: I just couldn't picture him with a needle and thread. He had these great big hands, he wore a gold watch and rings. I couldn't imagine him being able to measure and sew. He agreed with everything Blasto said; he just nodded and grinned. He didn't seem to have many ideas of his own. He didn't say much.

Goffo had a thing for me. He used to bring me flowers. He brought me a shirt once, sewn by his father; it was such soft cotton, sky-blue. Sometimes I like to wear it; I like the cloth on my skin, reminding me. I don't bear grudges. I like to tell the tale.

Blasto was scared I'd get into Carme's head. When she wasn't around he used to taunt me for working at Mickeys. He'd say it was a whorehouse.

'So how come you let Carme work there?' I asked one day as I stood in the kitchen chopping tomatoes. 'Because she keeps you? Because it pays for you? Eh?'

'That's enough, *signorina*,' he said.

He pointed a stubby finger into my face.

'Enough?' I repeated. 'Oh. I'm sorry.'

And I took my knife and cut swiftly into the fruit.

When Goffo asked me to go out with them all one night to some kind of Christmas dance, I watched Blasto flinch.

'Sure,' I said. 'I'd like that.'

Goffo beamed. Then he looked at Blasto and guffawed: 'She's fantastic! Isn't she fantastic?'

Blasto balked. I turned my back and left the room.

7

Goffo took us all to the *Palazzo Di Mare*: Catania's biggest dance hall. The *Palazzo* was notorious; it stretched majestic along the promenade, low and long and lit with real fire torches. From its windows – if it was clear – you could see Calabria: a cluster of dim, shimmering lights marking the mainland. But the night we went we had no such view: the tide was high; black breakers slapped the pier in a storm. Thin lines of foam danced white on the water. The moon was like a wheel in the sky.

We sat, six of us, at a table with a single candle. Blasto was restless. He was cutting at the candle with this little pocket-knife he had, letting wax drip on to his fingers and then scraping it off with the blade. Vito was hunched in his chair, slamming shorts. Goffo was smoking cigars and gawking at me between puffs. I was talking to Carme about nothing much; Laura was pointing over at the stage and giggling at the band.

'What's so funny?' Blasto snapped.

He took his eyes off the candle for a moment; hot wax ran on to the table and turned from clear to white.

'Nothing,' Laura answered – but she stopped at once.

I guess the band were pretty funny, but I liked them. It was old fifties tunes they were playing, real gangster music. The musicians were all dressed up; they had pencil moustaches and greased-back hair. Goffo sensed my happiness: he ordered champagne and we drank it from tall glasses. Then he asked me to dance and I said why not; I didn't see the harm. The only friends Goffo had were the ones he could buy and that made me sorry. He had blown his apprentice wages for the week on *Palazzo* tickets and drink. He bowed as I stood; he took my arm – and right then when he asked me to dance, I wanted to. But on the floor Goffo was nervous. He didn't know where to put his hands. He kept laughing and snorting, treading on my feet with his brogues. I was giddy, drunk on *Ferrari*. I was singing and whirling and forgetting my words; I kept saying things in English, getting all mixed up. It must have been a while before I noticed Goffo's shoulders stooping down, his hands clutching at my bones. Then him repeating my name as we circled the room:

'Marlena, Marlena. My girl from England, Marlena.'

'Enough,' I said. 'Let's enjoy the music.'

But he only said my name again; he lowered his mouth down to mine and gripped me tight. Poor, stupid Goffo. I didn't want to kiss him. I wriggled from his hold; I pushed him away. Then I walked back to Carme where she sat twisting her hair, left him standing there in the crowd with his oafish smile – wishing he'd find some other girl to feed his lonesome dreams.

Carme seemed drunk too. At least, she was laughing a lot. We talked for a while about things I don't remember. Then we walked across the room under the silver lights and stood at the bar. You could really see the band from there – see their make-up and spats and long, black-tipped shoes. I watched the spotlight shift round the singer as he moved from side to side; I saw the double bass twirl on its metal point. I had never been anywhere like that. I felt alive; I felt good. But then this bad thing happened and the night and the music slid into sadness and sourness. People are so predictable. They go round in circles. They have these mad patterns which they follow, which they trace and trace. I have only ever known one being whose pattern didn't seem just a wheel of sorrow to me. It was Jula, of course. Who else?

So we were standing at the bar and we were asking for vodka. Carme was telling me how the peroxide she used to dye her hair made her head bleed. Anyway, this Moroccan guy came over and started talking. He was tall and slim with a thin chain around his neck. His hair fell in oily ringlets down his back. He smiled a lot, this boy; he had a smile that was bright white. He wore blue jeans and a T-shirt that read *Come To America* – and he had these hands: hands like a pianist or a woman; they dangled around his body as he spoke in his three foreign languages: broken English, slow Italian, lilting French.

'Have you been to the States?' I asked.

He shook his head.

'No. Only here, to Sicily. And my own country, *Maroc*.'

So we started to talk about Morocco, about the things I had read in holiday magazines. I asked him about the souks and the desert sun, about the Sahara stretching right out to Timbuktu and beyond. He said: '*C'est un bel pays, mademoiselle. Un bel pays, oui.*' His voice dragging sweetly, like a song.

After a while the boy turned to Carme.

'What about you?' he said, smiling into her face. 'Have you ever desired to travel?'

'Oh well,' she said, out of the side of her mouth. She glanced about with worried eyes. 'I have always wanted to visit Poland.'

She bit her lip after she had spoken the word, as if she had uttered a betrayal.

'*Polonia?*' said the boy. His brown hands danced to the name.

'Yes,' Carme replied, trying to calm herself. 'One day I would like to go.'

And she started to talk the way she sometimes would in the club. She talked of the Polish mountains she had seen on the TV – and her face started to look different. She stuck her chin out like she did when she was happy, and I thought maybe we could be friends after all. But then Blasto came up behind us out of nowhere and grabbed Carme's arm. She cowered. The boy stepped back.

'*Ca-carino!*' Carme stammered. 'I was coming to find you!'

'No you weren't,' he said, tightening his grip.

He looked so short and stupid then, dressed up in his little black tux, with cream in his hair and his eyes so close together. I came and stood next to Carme. I noticed he was trying to grow a moustache.

'Leave her alone, Marlena!' Blasto whinged. Then he added: 'She's not your kind!'

'What do you mean by that?'

'She's not a junkie!' he shouted. People turned their heads. 'Look at you, don't say you're not! I can see it in you!'

His words fell between us. Faces watched me. For a moment I wished I could dissolve into the dark. Then heat rose in my cheeks, my hands, my lips. I laughed at Blasto. I spat at him.

'You know nothing about me,' I said.

'Bitch,' he spluttered, putting a handkerchief to his eye and pulling Carme away.

It's difficult for me to remember the rest of that night in the *Palazzo*. It all happened pretty quick. I remember the sharp way Blasto spoke as he took Carme out of earshot. I remember the desperate expression on Carme's face, how the Arab guy slipped through the crowd like a deer, his eyes flashing sadly at me as he looked over his shoulder, the blare of the band as it played on – and how Goffo was suddenly there again too, clutching at my hand and begging me to dance.

'Don't you listen?' I cried. 'Ask someone else, can't you?'

I walked away. I no longer cared about Goffo. I wanted to know what Blasto was saying to Carme. I followed him as he marched her across the room. Swaying couples moved to let me pass as he led her out of a fire door and down an alley at the side of the hall. It was wet outside, raining hard. I walked softly, stopping dead when I saw Blasto push Carme up against the *Palazzo* wall.

'You're a slut!' he shouted. 'You want to be a nigger's girl!'

And he kicked at the ground with his boot saying: 'A nigger's girl! A nigger's girl! You want to be a nigger's girl!'

Water streamed down Carme's face. She stayed quiet. She slumped limp against the alley wall. In the gaps when Blasto stopped his chant I heard the pounding of the sea.

'Isn't that right?' he screamed. '*Isn't that right?*'

He seemed insane to me now; he sounded mad. When Carme dared to answer, 'No,' he jumped up and head-butted the air. Then he raised his hand in a fist and punched her face: once, twice. He yanked her hair back from her head as she screamed no again – and called her Liar! Liar! Liar! until there was nothing left for her to do but fall to the ground, sobbing in the downpour.

8

Thirty years ago there were hardly any Romanies in Sicily. Few went so far south. They settled mainly in the north – they weren't the kind you get now; for sure, they weren't the urban gypsies. And they weren't the rare half-breeds like Jula. These were the old Roma, the ones that are just rumours nowadays; the knife-sharpeners, the fortune-tellers, the ones you hear about but can't find. None of them spoke Italian. They didn't have cars or apartments or mobile phones. They lived in wagons; they bought and sold horses. They came and found work on the mandarin groves. Sometimes on a market day you would see them hanging around in twos or threes down in the towns. Mostly, though, they kept their distance and camped up high.

In Taormina they took a patch of land just off the road to Castelmola. You could see it from the open-air theatre: an S-shaped stretch running the length of the cliff. It was a few miles out of town – and way above it, like a kingdom's top. Standing up there in the grasses you could see the cars going up and down on the Messina highway. Ahead of you was the sea, *L'Isola Bella*; the jagged black rocks of the coast playing hide-and-seek with the tide. At the southern end of the old gypsy site you could gaze down into the theatre-bowl, where tourists roamed microscopic between the firs and ancient stones. You could scan Taormina's rooftops: all whitewash and terracotta, TV aerials, satellite dishes, laundry lines.

Of course the site had changed. There were no gypsies now. It was just a field of red and yellow poppies. Jula took me there. The first things we saw as we climbed the Castelmola road were a row of shabby olive stalls lining the bank and a guy selling Taormina hats out the back of a van. Around the next bend was a bar; Jula said it was pretty new. He stopped the truck when we reached it. The sign above the door hung on painted chains. It read DEGLI ZINGARI. We went inside. It was like a joke; it was bright and badly lit – and everything was fake. Weird wood-print paper covered the walls, there were plastic roses on all the tables – and a list of novelty cocktails was chalked up on a board. *Try our Lucky Shoe. Our Gypsy Bride. Sample our Crystal Ball.*

Jula and I ordered straight *gingerini* and drank them with lemon chunks. I bought cigarettes from the *padrone*; I tried to talk to him. But he had nothing to say to me; he thumbed through a book of puzzles as I spoke, chewing on a pencil-end.

'What's with the questions?' he snapped, when I asked him about the gypsies. He started doing a crossword. 'Haven't you got a better place to be?'

'I've come to see the old site,' I told him.

'Sure. The old site. The field.'

He printed the word POMODORO into his crossword grid.

'Don't bother, *carina. Sono tutti malefici.* They're parasites too. Go to the new place if you want to learn.'

'Why do you have to call them parasites?'

'Why do you not?' He spat out a piece of gnawed wood. 'Been here long, *signorina*? All they do is beg and breed.'

36

I turned to see Jula laughing as he sat facing me in a fake wood booth. He downed his drink, fished out his lemon slice with two fingers and sucked on it until it made him smart. We left the *padrone* to his brainteasers. We walked out the back entrance on to the plain.

'What a jerk,' Jula said as we waded through long grass.

'Where's the new site?' I asked.

'At the river.'

'How long's it been there?'

'Years. The mayor had them all moved on from here when the tourist thing really started up. Some of them stayed, some of them are still here. But most of them left town.'

Jula skimmed the grass-tops with his palms, back and forth.

'Did your father stay?' I asked, tentative.

'No.'

He walked away from me then. He went along the slopes and towards the theatre-top. Down in Taormina church bells sounded. Jula stumbled in the grass.

'Look!' he cried.

I ran to him. He had found an old tethering peg. He was squatting over it, trying to pull it from the ground. After a few attempts it loosened, then it came out altogether. Pale soil filled the new hole. Jula fell back. The peg was made from iron and hammer-marked, maybe a foot long. It was rusting at one end; at the other it was silver-black. He stood up and beheld it.

'The last thing,' he said.

I looked down at it, quizzical.

'What?'

'On the old site, Marlena – this is how they tied their horses. This could be all there is left of them, imagine that! The last thing!'

We walked; Jula carried the peg. At the north edge of the plain we came to a fence. We sat down then, knees-to-chest, our backs to the fence-posts and chicken-wire. Grass-heads brushed our skin. Jula struck the peg lightly on a stone. It made a short, flat note, not quite music.

'Still, I can't keep it,' he said to himself. 'It's not mine.'

I guess I didn't really know what Jula wanted on that day. I just followed him – into the bar, along the strip, down to the peg. Before we returned to the truck he searched again for the hole. He followed our grass tracks. He went on ahead. It didn't take him long; he trod swiftly, soft, signalling to me with a raised hand as he found the small patch of sunken earth and – quick, unceremonious – he pushed the tethering peg back.

9

I didn't return to the *Palazzo* after I had seen Blasto beat Carme. I doubled back down the alley, walked along the seafront and caught the late bus home. I felt queasy with it all; my head was swimming. When I got back to the tenement I watched TV. I drank a glass of wine. Then I went to bed and stared up at the ceiling where images of the night floated relentless before my eyes.

I was just drifting off to sleep when my door opened. A thin shaft of light fell into the room. I saw the bulk of a man standing there with his head hanging down. It was Goffo.

'It's OK,' he whispered. 'It's only me.'

I was dazed, the way you are when you jolt fast out of dreams.

'What do you want?' I asked. 'What are you doing here?'

'Blasto gave me the keys,' he said. 'He told me to take care of you.'

'*What?*'

He came and kneeled beside the bed.

Goffo didn't say anything else. He drew in his breath and began to kiss my face. He climbed on top of me and pushed his tongue into my mouth. He had sour breath; his lips were cracked. I tried to speak but he pushed down hard with his stupid neck and jaw. Then he pushed with his body, too, pulled the sheets away from me and said: 'I love you, Marlena.'

I let myself wilt under his weight.

'I said I love you,' he repeated.

I played dead. I waited for him to give up. I watched the fan whirr above us, felt the cool gold of Goffo's crucifix dangling on to my collarbone as he mauled my face with his mouth. Then I gaped at him as he lifted himself from me and started to unhook his belt. Anger throbbed in my fingers.

'Get out!' I shouted.

'But Marlena!' he cried, pulling at my shirt.

I slapped him hard on the side of his face.

'I said get out!'

Goffo froze – seconds passed – then he put his head in his hands and started to cry. Italian men are just like that.

'I'm sorry,' he said. 'I'm so lonely!'

'So change the company you keep,' I snapped. 'And fuck off!'

He looked at me with baby eyes.

'You don't understand me,' he muttered. He did up his trousers and stumbled away from the bed. 'Maybe I'll see you tomorrow?' he said. '*O forse dopodomani*?'

He edged towards the door, his eyes still pleading.

Once he had turned his back I lay down again; I rolled over and faced the wall. Along the hall I heard laughter; Blasto and Carme were coming home. They must have made things up, I thought. Soon they would be making their weird love. I stared into the dull light of my room: red every seventh second. I cursed Monte Tesoro. I wished Etna would shoot fire into the sky. But wishing was no good. I had to make plans. Even before Goffo had closed the door I had begun thinking of a way out.

10

Finding a new place was pretty easy. Maybe it's my face or something. I just went to Libost every night – I worked the afternoon shift at Mickeys then headed downtown to the club. I wore lipstick. I stood at the bar and ate peanuts. I wasn't looking for any new romance – the thing with Goffo had put me off. And although I scoured the crowds for Jula each night, my heart deep rhythm-dancing in my chest, he was nowhere to be seen.

I tried the women first, which turned out to be a waste of time. You can't make friends with Italian women. You can't start asking them if they know of any cheap rooms. They come out in droves, all the Francescas and Marias and Margheritas. They have perfect faces; they talk in code. And if they do happen to notice you – because you're before them at the bar or in front of them at a queue for the bathroom mirror – they only hate you for your blue eyes; they only sneer and say *Scusi*. If you're not a sister or an aunt or a niece or a brother's girlfriend then forget it. You're outside their circle. You don't exist.

So I got in with a few of the local boys, the ones who hung out on the club balcony and smoked dope. They weren't so bad; they didn't seem to mind me being around. But they were all so young, and it turned out most of them were homeless, spending all night on the streets or sleeping on floors. I started thinking maybe Libost wasn't the place to look. I wondered if Mickey might put me up – but then I thought of the cost. According to the other girls who worked out at the bar, Mickey's price for favours was high.

Then, just when I had stopped hoping, it happened. One misty night at the start of November, I was staring hapless into the bar mirror and at the spirit bottles all upside down and in a row, when I saw someone staring back. He was tall, he was pretty-faced; he was curly-headed and dressed up smart. His eyes were this pale, limpid green. I stood and watched as he threw me an idiot grin and leaned across me to scoop up a handful of nuts. In pure relief, I grinned back. I could smell his cleanness behind me, his freshness; that strange, chemical mixture of laundry powder, soap and aftershave which all the rich boys have.

'*Ciao alla rossa-bionda,*' he said, crunching.

I turned around and faced him square. He was my cue.

11

Paolo was all right. I mean, it was true what Jula said: he was *borghese*. He was small-minded, middle-class and uptight. All his problems came from his being wealthy, Jula told me. Maybe he was right. His family were from Taormina's richest quarter; they were women, mostly. They still all lived there together in a gaggle, pecking and flapping and fighting up in one of the grand sandstone villas that overlooked the rest of the town.

There were eight of them. They all had the same look. Three sisters, two young nieces, a fat, sweating aunt, the *nonna*. Out of all the Zeppellis I liked her best. She was little and bony; she had a loud mouth and a crazy laugh and even when she was clean she stank like a wild pig. *nonna* was old – and mad; she used to dance on the villa stairs. She combed her fine, white hair with any toothbrush she could find and heaped the Zeppelli table cutlery under her bed. She was smart too. She said I was a hooker. She used to mumble it under her breath whenever I was around, showing her shrunken gums and rotten teeth: '*La bottana! Che bottana! Esci fuori da qui! Bottana!*'

I didn't care what she said. She was so crazy. Some days she nagged me and called me the name of her dead husband. On others she would squeal with delight when I walked in the door, put her cold, withered hands to my cheeks and declare I had the face of a virgin saint.

The only guy in the house was *zio*. He was all muscle and gloom. It was true, he was getting old but I could see that once he had been a real man. His hands were covered in long black hairs; he had a fat commander's nose which was bent from a bad break. Paolo said he had been to war. By the time I met him, though, he just watched quiz show TV all day. Whenever I visited the villa I used to sit with him and do the same.

Sometimes I would catch *zio* looking at me like he might have looked at a girl forty years ago. He had these big, eager eyes for me. He used to stare at my body, my bones. And if ever I chose to look back at him he would cast his eyes down and turn back to the screen. He didn't need to do that; I didn't mind him looking. In the darkness of the lounge I liked to let him watch. We had something in common, after all. On those slow afternoons together we were hiding from the world.

Our refuge never lasted. It was only ever a matter of time before *zia* – Paolo's hideous aunt – came slouching down the hall in her flip-flops to glare at me and whack *zio* around the back of the head for not answering the series of questions she bellowed from the other room. She was such a bully. Once I saw her hit *zio* with a shoe. She caught his ear with the heel-tip; she made it bleed. He didn't make a sound when it happened; he didn't even look round. He just took a handkerchief from his shirt pocket and stemmed the flow.

Once Paolo had finished school in Taormina he left the family villa. He moved to Catania and took a university place. A big job in Milan was what he said he wanted; a flash car and a heap of cash.

'To keep us rich!' *zia* used to say. 'That's why he abandoned us all!'

I couldn't work out if that was a joke. I don't think it was. I think *zia* really did worry about who would keep her rich now that *zio* was ageing. Who would keep her in bad dresses and leg wax. Every once in a while the Zeppelli women would cram themselves into the family car and visit Paolo in his flat. I don't know why they bothered; it was a thirty-kilometre drive south to Catania and they all hated Via Soreca. It backed right on to the immigrant quarter – and on to the railway, too, where the Arabs and blacks spilled out of their homes to spread their cigarettes or leather or carvings or whatever it was they had to sell out on the grassy banks between the train tracks and the road. *Zia* said it was a dirty neighbourhood. It wasn't right for Paolo, she grumbled. It wasn't clean. She tutted at his broken mailbox; she wouldn't sit down in his house. She lifted her nose in disgust each time she staggered down the pissy halls.

'It suits me, *zia*,' Paolo used to say in a tight voice. 'For one thing, it's cheap!'

But then he would bring out his screwdriver after she had gone and have another go at fixing the mailbox hinge; fill up his old black bucket with water and bleach and try to choke the smell of urine rising from the marble floors.

1 2

The best thing about Paolo was his motorbike. He had a new Ducati 748. Everyone gives you something – and those high-speed rides clutching on to his back, zooming along cliffs in winter winds, in spring thunderstorms with my hair stuck down on to my skull – those freedom rides were the gifts Paolo gave to me. He showed me Sicily's grand vistas, the amphitheatres, the ruins. He took me to the mountains, the markets; to the village kiosks selling sweet mandarin juice served in a salt-rimmed glass. Any chance I got I asked him to take me out. Things might have been different if we could have forever ridden the bike.

Paolo loved to go back to Taormina. It was where he grew up. I remember the first time he took me there. We sped down through the old town to the best restaurant he knew. He asked for the table with the best sea view – then he ordered stuffed black olives on sticks, grilled swordfish steaks and blood oranges in oil.

'The real Sicily!' he said, grinning at me as the food arrived.

He was rolling a cocktail stick between teeth. That was Paolo all over: he was a veneer, a cut-out, he was all show. When we fucked for the first time that night he lit candles. He undressed me with a ceremony I found absurd. Then when it was over he cried into my hair for his dead *mamma*. I half-expected him then to announce it again: 'The real Sicily!'

Maybe I'm cruel. I guess most women would love all those dinners and dates. Candles and cards and roses in tubes. It must be me. Still, Paolo was all right. He let me stay in his flat. And for a while, at least, that was enough.

13

'You can't wear that!' Paolo squealed when he first saw my favourite dress.

It's my rose dress; it's thin and dark and covered in thorns and blooms; they cascade in garlands over my knees. It's so old now that it's falling apart – but I could never throw it out. Whenever I see a new hole starting to appear – those tiny criss-cross threads revealing skin – I sew it up myself.

We were in the bedroom at Via Soreca. I was standing up on tiptoes searching for a cotton reel. It was a Sunday; church bells were ringing. We were going to Taormina to see *zia*.

'It's not right,' said Paolo. 'It makes you look like *una sciattona*!'

I jumped down from the chair.

'I can't find it.'

'Find what?'

'I was going to mend my dress; see this new hole at my thigh? Now I'm not. I can't find my cotton. I'm ready, Paolo. Let's go.'

So I turned up in my old rose dress and of course they all stared. They passed the plates around the table like we were at a funeral tea. They shuffled in their seats and coughed and looked stiff. It didn't matter what I said to them, they just couldn't seem to smile. They talked about decency and fashion. They remarked upon what one does and doesn't do. Paolo's sisters had always had it in for me, right from the start – and that day they were just like serpents, hissing and tangling their arms together as they made jokes in the hall. *Zia* was no better. It was obvious what she thought. All through the meal she asked questions about me in a loud, hollow voice – but she wouldn't look into my eyes or talk to me direct.

'Does she have a proper job yet?' she boomed at Paolo.

She bit into a large lump of gristle and had to spit it on to her plate. She grabbed at her glass of wine and gulped, dribbling purple down her chin.

'I told you,' I interrupted.

'*Or is she relying on you?*'

'You must have forgotten,' I said. 'I'm a . . .'

'Waitress,' said Paolo.

He nudged me under the table like the coward that he was. I took my boot heel then and trod down hard on to his foot.

'Why don't you play us something at the piano?' Paolo asked, once the food was gone. I could feel the silence eating into him, forcing him to talk. The big pendulum clock began to chime.

'Come on, *moglie*,' he persisted. 'Entertain me!'

Now when someone asks me to play piano for them like that I just won't do it. I'm not a machine. I won't jump. But I felt like showing the Zeppelli family something that Sunday afternoon. I finished my drink and got up; in my rose dress I walked over to the piano like a queen. It was covered in dust and made from mahogany: a beautiful instrument as it happens – and I sat down and played 'Clair de lune' with no music there in front of me, no nothing. I closed my eyes; I bent my body over the keys and pushed my soul out into the parochial air. I love Debussy. I love his 'Clair de lune'. It's like looking out of your window to see the world covered in snow; it's like being pure again. It's the sound of water, falling; it's a deep, soft dream.

'She's a whore!' cried the *nonna* in my last note's echo.

Zia couldn't help herself; she laughed a spiteful laugh. I raised my foot from the pedal, lifted my hands from the keys and opened up my eyes. *Nonna* had taken me by surprise. She was standing right next to me with her hands on her hips, moving her body from side to side and blowing kisses at me like a street girl. Then she laughed too, high-pitched and insane.

'A whore! A whore!' was her lunatic eulogy.

She was so close I could smell the madness on her breath. I shut the piano lid. Then I looked up at *nonna* and I smiled.

Once the plates were cleared from the table Paolo went through to the kitchen to talk to his sisters. I crept down to the TV room.

'I like the way you play,' said *zio* as I walked in.

He was sitting in his armchair. He looked like a dying man. The TV screen was making lights and shadows flicker across his luckless face.

'Thanks,' I said.

We turned to face the show. Women in pink bikinis span a golden wheel. As usual, after a few minutes, *zio*'s eyes had wandered from them. He wanted to look at me. But when I returned his glance, he bowed his head.

'Don't look away,' I said. 'Please, *zio*. Don't look away.'

He faced me now. I had called him Uncle. We sat eye to eye. I thought about *zia*: her face, her cruel words. I thought about Paolo: he was nothing but a spineless fool.

Taking a breath I walked over to *zio* and kneeled in front of him. I slipped the straps of my rose dress down over my shoulders. I was naked to the waist. He leaned forward. He was trembling; there were tears in his milky eyes. Neither of us said anything. Neither of us moved. We just stayed there, motionless, in the silence until *zia* came padding down the hall moaning about the meat scraps having been thrown away, and could *zio* not have thought before he was so stupid as to have chucked them in the *spazza*? Why the devil had she married him? She was sure she didn't know.

Her hand reached the doorknob. At the sight of her bulk filling the pane of frosted glass, I stood up. I pulled up my dress and sat down on a chair. *Zia* strode in; I faced the TV. Zio's time was up. The spell had been broken. And my heart was pounding with gladness at what I had done.

14

'You should have worn what I told you!' Paolo complained as we left the villa.

He was sitting on the Ducati, his voice muffled by his helmet. I hitched up my dress and climbed on to the bike. He revved the engine; we rumbled down cobbled streets. When we reached the main road lights, he turned his head.

'You should have done what I told you!' he shouted again through the visor.

'I can't hear you,' I said.

We got home late to dark rooms. We ate cold meats. We watched TV. Later – on the floor, with some bad B-movie playing – we fucked. He moved over me: I couldn't stand it; I had to turn my face away. I screwed up my eyes and clenched my teeth and when he came – moaning *Madonna*! – I dug my nails into his skin.

'You scratched me!' he simpered afterwards, twisting like a girl in the mirror to study the marks.

I glanced up from the TV; he pouted.

'It hurt! Don't do it again!'

I switched channels. There was only trash to watch. I looked over at Paolo's back. Three thin, hot lines ran the length of his torso – from his hairless neck to the dark base of his spine.

'Did you *mean* to do it? Did you *mean* to draw blood?'

I threw him a dry smile. I was starting to wish I hadn't moved in. Lying there on the kitchen floor, watching Paolo nurse his petty wounds, I all but hated him.

A few hours later the buzzer went. It was past midnight; Paolo was sleeping. I got out of bed and slung on my dress. I walked on to the balcony. I hung my head over the rail and peered down into streetlight. Suddenly a man in a bomber jacket stepped back into the road and looked up at me.

'Hello, pretty one,' he said.

He was tall and poised. Maybe I even thought he was handsome. He had these big, sulky lips and a neat black goatee.

'I've heard all about you,' he shouted. 'You must be Marlena.'

He clicked his heels together. I waited for him to say who he was.

'Well?' he asked. 'Aren't you going to let me in?'

His accent was familiar. I couldn't think exactly how. I went down to the door barefoot and slid open the steel bolts. Pulling it open a crack I looked out. He was much taller than me, this guy; he was well over six-foot. He was broad, too.

'Paolo in?' he said.

'No. I mean, he's sleeping.'

'Worn him out, eh?'

'What's that supposed to mean?'

'My little darling, it is not supposed to mean *anything*. Now, did I wake you from your slumbers? If I did, I do apologize.'

He took my hand and kissed it.

'I wasn't asleep,' I said, pulling my arm back.

He looked me up and down as if he might have been thinking about buying a horse.

'Wake Paolo,' he said. He held up a bag of beer. 'He'll be pleased to see me, eh? He won't mind.'

He winked at me and clicked his heels again. I stepped back as he walked into the hall. I turned around. He pushed the door shut. Then he followed me upstairs.

Paolo was pleased to see the tall guy. He woke up immediately and put on his gown. I went back to bed; they sat in the kitchen and began drinking. I lay there under the covers, listening to them crack jokes through the wall. I couldn't tell what they were saying – but Paolo's tone was new to me. He sounded like one kid trying to impress another, unsure of himself.

'Who was that?' I asked when he returned to the bedroom. 'And what have you been saying to him? Who was he? How did he know my name?'

The night was almost over by then. Daylight pushed through the shutters. Paolo stank of beer. He belched loudly and pulled off his gown; he threw himself on to the bed.

'Savio? He's an old friend. He lives up on Etna. At the Schigghiapeddi farm.'

I leaned up on one elbow, alert.

'The Schigghiapeddi farm? Does he know Jula?'

'Of course he knows Jula! He's Jula's brother! He doesn't *like* him,' he ranted. 'But then, who *does* like their kin? So you've met him, eh? Jula! Sly bastard, he puts himself around! What was he doing with you?'

I didn't answer.

'Where did you meet him, Marlena?'

'I just saw him in Libost one night,' I said.

I wanted Paolo to shut up.

'And don't tell me, he tried to fuck you!'

'No, that was you. When I met *you* in Libost, *you* tried to fuck me.'

'I did fuck you,' he laughed. 'It was easy!'

'Is that what you told Savio?'

Paolo sniggered. He climbed on top of me and started rolling around.

'Come on, Marlena. Give me more of that Lupone passion!'

'Fuck off,' I said. 'Fuck off.'

15

Of course Savio wasn't exactly Jula's brother; I knew that. He was his half-brother. He liked to make it known. I remember when I first heard him say it; how his words sliced the air. He pursed his thick lips and petted his beard.

'*Il mio fratellastro*,' he announced. '*Il bastardo*.'

It had been another night in at Via Soreca. Savio and Paolo and a few guys from Paolo's course were sitting round the table playing cards. They were playing *scopa*. It was for money that evening, just change at first – but Savio kept upping the ante. He wouldn't stop. When the stakes passed fifty thousand lire, one of the student guys – this tubby kid with a ring in his lip – laid down his cards. He shook his head and said he didn't have the cash. The guy next to him folded too – then Paolo quit. Savio called them all faggots.

'Let's go to the harbour,' the fat boy said. 'Watch the ships come in.'

'And the hookers come out! Let's go get 'em!' cried Paolo, as if he screwed whores all the time.

When the boys left in their jackets and hats I went with them. I was glad to get out of the flat. It was raining on the waterfront: there were no hookers, no returning ships. The boats were still and brightly-lit, anchored together in a row by the far wall of the quay. A storm was coming. Foam teemed in on the breakers; the ocean moaned. The boys lit cigarettes, despondent; they pulled their hoods over their heads. I walked towards the pier-end where the waves were slap-slapping the stone. I pushed my hands into my pockets and shook down my damp hair. I felt thankful, somehow, at the water-edge; I could have stayed on the docks for hours – but after just a few minutes I heard a high-pitched noise in the wind. It was Savio, on the far quayside, with his fingers in his mouth. He was whistling me back like a dog; then he was yelling: 'We're sick of this now! It's pissing down! Time to smoke some hash!'

My hair blew over my cheeks and eyes. I was so bored of what they did. I mouthed my boredom to the sea. Then with the taste of salt on my lips, I followed them.

Paolo made tea when we got in. For a while I was content – the way you are when you come in from the cold. I sat on the floor and dried my hair with a towel; I flicked through some of Paolo's books. But then the guys started talking about a superman, a super-race; about Nietzsche, all that philosophy stuff. Someone nudged me on the elbow.

'Hey, Marlena, the *Übermensch*, what do you think about that?'

'I don't know,' I shrugged. It was true. I didn't. 'All I know about Nietzsche is that he cried for a horse.'

'What?'

'What are you talking about?'

'He saw a horse being lashed in the street. He cried for it.'

'Why did he do that?' asked the tubby guy.

'He broke down in tears at the sight of its blood. He never recovered; he just kept on crying. After that day he went gradually mad.'

'Why are you talking about horses?' asked Paolo. 'How do you know all that, Marlena?'

'This professor I knew told me.'

'What professors have you ever known?' he scoffed.

I looked at him, blank.

'Just forget it.'

After that I kind of lost the thread. They were all talking so fast and interrupting each other; in the end I couldn't keep up. It was textbook talk in any case; it wasn't real to me. I wished they would talk about something else. I went on to the balcony. The rain was pouring down. For a long time I watched the drops of water streak silver in the light. The bar below us was closed now – but the sign was still flashing:

BIBITE BIBITE

On, off. On, off. I counted: a single second between each flash. Then something else – familiar, irregular; something coming from inside. It stood out in the drone of words like a signal: Jula, Jula. Jula, Jula. And again I heard it: Jula.

'What are you talking about?' I shouted.

Savio turned his head. 'My half-brother. The bastard!'

'Come on,' said Paolo. 'Jula's OK.'

'He's gypsy!' Savio retorted. 'Gypsies are cretins, they're animals!'

'No, man,' said the tubby guy.

'You know it's true.'

'Maybe they're half-cretins!' Paolo spluttered. 'Half-beasts!'

Savio nodded in approval at the gag and jeered: 'Marlena, isn't that so?'

A line of yellow-brown smoke streamed from his lips; I turned back and faced the rain.

Maybe I would have left Paolo then, if I'd thought hard enough – but I got distracted; I forgot about it: down at the bar something was going on. A white Mercedes had pulled up in the street. Male heads were moving around the boot. I heard footsteps; whispers. I saw boxes being passed. Deftly, noiselessly; from one pair of hands to another: out the back of the car, up the bar steps and out of sight. I counted the boxes as they went by; there were twenty-five. The same size, the same colour. I wondered what they held. I guessed heroin. I guessed cocaine. I guessed guns.

I watched the heads and the hands and the boxes until a bald guy with a mark on his head slammed the car boot shut. I leaned down close; I half-balanced on my belly over the rail. It was a birthmark there on the top of his head. It was funny – from that angle it looked like a little heart. The men disappeared. I heard the bar door being locked behind them. A few moments later the Merc drove away. The birthmark man was gone. The street was empty again.

All the time I had been watching my blood was rushing in my veins. Now I grew calm, like I had drunk a double shot. I smiled on to the deserted road. Paolo had always told me to keep away from there – but then, what did he know?

'*Don't get involved in things!*' he would shout theatrically, his eyes widening so much that he looked like a toad.

Sometimes I just said what he wanted to hear. 'I won't,' was always my reply. 'Honestly, Paolo – why would I?' But nobody had seen me. Those guys were only doing what they did. They weren't thinking about any English girl six feet above them; it was fine. Paolo was uptight, just like Jula said. No one knew I was watching them. Nobody ever looked up.

16

Jula hadn't always been a joke to Paolo. They shared a common past. When Paolo and I were alone at night, when he had loosened his shoulders after a couple of beers, laid down his guard – then he would tell me the tales. I used to lie there in bed listening to him talking, creating shadow-pictures on the walls as he gestured to me about this time with Jula and that.

They were the same age, born in the same summer month. They had the same friends; they went to the same school. They were even delivered by the same midwife, who rode on her bike all the way from Gaggi to birth them: Jula on the kitchen table up at the farm; Paolo a week later in an old oak bed down in Taormina town.

'Jula didn't cry when he was born,' Paolo told me. 'But me, I screamed and screamed!'

It figured. Paolo was always making a noise. Mostly I learned to shut his voice out. But on the nights when he spoke about Jula I'd sit up and pay attention.

'Tell me the fire story,' I'd say. 'It's my favourite one.'

Paolo could never understand my interest. Only a mad girl would choose Jula, he said. He had no bank account, no job; he didn't even have a watch. He deserted from his military service after a week – and spent the year on the gypsy site! What man would do that? No girl would count on Jula. He was an unsafe bet.

Still, Paolo told the story. In spite of himself, he told it. He was as drawn to Jula as I was; he just couldn't say it. He didn't have the balls.

One night after school Jula and Paolo went down to the *spiagge nascoste* – the hidden beaches, to the south of town. It was one of those summers when they did everything together. They were never apart – and never at home. They would sit on street corners trading football cards and tricks; they hung around at the entrances of bars. *Zia* didn't like it. She was afraid Paolo might learn to smoke and swear. He was already playing backgammon for change in the playground. She took the money from him, saying it was immoral. She tried to keep Paolo indoors. The thing is, she had no real reason to object – until the night of the fire.

On that night they swapped clothes for a joke. They sat on the sand playing jacks and waiting for dark. When the sun went down behind the line of the sea Jula collected wood and built a bonfire on the shore. Crabs scuttled into the darkness. Waves came lapping around the flames. It must have been a crazy sight all right: Jula standing in the firelight, dressed in Paolo's school blazer and shorts. Paolo, for once free of his suit, doing a crab-dance around the pit and laughing with glee at the feel of being clothed in Jula's blouse, bandanna and jeans.

'You can't imagine!' whispered Paolo, his hand-shapes blazing upon the wall.

Then things went wrong. Jula got bored and took a stick from the ground. He wrapped Paolo's breast-pocket handkerchief around one end and doused the thing in whisky. He always carried a flask of something, even when I knew him. Anyway, he had this torch now – and he was holding it high in the air like he was leading a mob.

He yelled over to Paolo and Paolo scampered after him, nervous, stammering, 'Hey, Jula, what's going on?' – as Jula ignored him and climbed up on to the grass banks behind the eucalyptus trees. All the plants up there were sun-scorched; dry. Jula knew that. He smiled at Paolo and lowered the torch to the ground.

The fire moved along the bank like a river in a storm. It spread its colours up the hill. Trees split and crackled; whole branches fell. It moved faster and faster: bright, raging heat. Jula watched it, mesmerized. He loved risk – and there were houses near, most hidden from sight, on the *scala*: the thousand steps which connected the beach with the road. Suddenly Paolo gasped in horror. Then Jula snapped to, screaming, 'Jesus! Fuck!' as the flames reached the *scala* fence – and old Nikki Battisti's barn.

From a distance the barn seemed to explode. Smoke mushroomed into the sky. For a moment Jula and Paolo were unable to move – then they ran, coughing and shouting until they reached the side of the road where they collapsed on to a grit pile, swearing on that bed of stones to keep it secret; to never tell a living soul. But the pact was pointless. When Nikki Battisti saw the fire from his house he ran out on to the far edge of the cliff. He could see clearly – the beach was bathed in light – and he could make out a figure bolting into the undergrowth. A boy in a gypsy blouse and black bandanna. No other kid dressed like that in town.

'It felt like the universe was ending that night!' Paolo told me as he turned out the light.

He reached out for my body then, trying to put his world back together. I turned to the wall.

The morning after the fire the whole of Taormina knew Jula had done it. Once the thing was put out, Nikki Battisti –

one of the town's chief winemakers then – rode on his donkey up to the farm. Jula didn't deny it; he was no liar. But he never mentioned Paolo.

'I lit a torch. It went wrong,' he kept saying. 'It took over. It had a will all its own!'

It was the talk of the foothills for a week or so – then people got over it. Even Nikki calmed down in the end. He didn't use the barn much in any case. There had been a few old wine vats in there, that was all. Yeah, Nikki forgave Jula. He didn't mean to do it. Jula was just a boy. He was fatherless, too. The truth was, Nikki liked him.

'If you want to make it up to me, *figlio*, you can help me in the vineyards,' he rasped, a cigarette between his teeth.

So Jula trod grapes all summer on the *scala*, until his toes turned red with the wine. His toenails turned red too, like he had painted them. But *zia* insisted it was a disgrace. She padded around Taormina calling Jula a hooligan. Worse, she told everyone Nikki was queer. She must have known Paolo was there that night. She would have smelled the woodsmoke on his clothes, for sure. But she never spoke of it to him. She just forbade him to have anything more to do with Jula. She met him at school each day, took his arm and pushed him home. Paolo did what he was told of course; he never spoke to Jula again. He stayed on the school grounds at break; he stopped smoking. He tried to make new friends. When Jula passed by, he sloped away to linger around the other boys. It didn't take him long to find another kid to cling to.

Savio was three years older than Paolo. In Paolo's school photos he stood out; towering high above the other boys, looking like he might salute at any moment and sticking his jaw out in a sneer. He was going to be a soldier was what he said. He brought toy guns to school, he fought; he talked military-talk all the time. And he ranted constantly about how much he hated Jula.

He used to strut around the schoolyard, telling the other kids Jula was gypsy. He threw stones at Jula, kicked his shoes. He bit him, too, once – on the chest, like a big cat – bit him all the way through his blouse. He leapt on him, snorting and snarling and leaving a set of purple-blue marks. All because Jula had won a prize: a cup for painting with his name etched on.

Paolo saw that fight. He saw Savio's mouth smeared with Jula's blood. He didn't protest; he just froze with fear. When Savio was finished, the younger boys came and kicked dust in Jula's eyes; then on Savio's command Paolo took the cup and threw it into the nettle-grass.

I can see right through most of the men I meet. And for all Paolo said on those nights, talking in bed in the back room at Via Soreca, I knew he was unable to forget. He remembered Jula and he loved him. We are our past; we are born from it. Without it we are nothing.

17

I had only been at Via Soreca a couple of months when the kids from upstairs attacked me. At least, that's what Paolo said it was: an attack. I'm not saying it didn't bother me; it left a sour taste in my mouth for days. But Paolo made it something it wasn't. He blew it out of all proportion.

It was a Saturday, some time after Christmas. It was a cold morning; the pavements were wet with rain. Paolo had been down to the market to buy breakfast. He'd brought back eggs, each one wrapped in paper. He had brought smoked meat and coffee. But he had forgotten the bread. He banged his fist on the table; he looked like he was about to cry.

'*Madonna mia!*' he whined.

'I'll go,' I said.

So I dressed and went out. I didn't want to eat with him in any case. I took the backstreets to the nearest baker and chose a hot new loaf. It was still early; as I left the shop with the bread under my arm, I looked up at the tenement buildings; all the shutters were closed. I breathed in deep; there was no one about. It made me feel I knew secrets.

Suddenly I heard voices around me. They were male voices, young. I looked over my shoulder and saw a cluster of faces at my back. It was the kids from our building. They were singing a little song.

The song was mean. It was in Czech Romani, I think –
that mix of sound-worlds; of blood. I didn't understand
the words – but the way they sang it, it sounded like an
insult. Like a joke at my expense.

'What do you want?' I asked.

Nobody spoke. The eldest boy laughed and clapped his
hands above his head. He had a mole above his lip; he
wore a bright yellow jacket with the collar turned up. It
made him look like a little gangster. He smirked at me.

'*Bílá! Bílá!*' he jeered.

The others shouted it too: '*Bílá! Bílá!*' They pointed at
my arms and legs.

'What do you want?' I said again.

'*Bílá! Bílá!*'

Then suddenly I understood. White. White. I faced the
boy in yellow. For a second time he said nothing; his eyes
widened to black pools. I set off again; the chant resounded.
I quickened my pace.

Then the stones began. At first they were small and
thrown low. Some missed me and rolled into the gutter;
others peppered my ankles and calves. They kept on coming; they didn't stop. Tears rose in my throat. My cheeks
burned. I should have yelled at them or fought back or
something – but I didn't. I hitched up my skirt. I took my
shoes off and held them by the straps and, from a gang of
boys no more than nine or ten years old, I ran.

The kids ran too; they were fast. I could feel them
gaining on me. They were louder now, bolder; the stones
were getting bigger. They were hitting my back and my
arms; they were hurting. When one struck my neck I cried
out and dropped the bread. The boys scrambled to pick it
up. I glanced behind me to see them tossing the loaf into
the air. The yellow boy whooped. He took a final stone
and flung it. I ducked, but it was too late; it caught my

eye. With my hand up around my brow I turned the corner, running. I knew they had stopped chasing me. But I ran until I reached Via Soreca. I unlocked the main door with shaky hands, slammed it behind me and staggered up the stairs.

'What happened to you?'

Paolo was sitting with his sunglasses on his head, chewing fried bacon.

'Where's the bread?'

'I lost it. Nothing happened. It was nothing. Just the kids from upstairs.'

He stood up. I wiped my eye with the back of my hand. It stung; my skin smeared red.

'Oh,' I said. 'I'm bleeding.'

'Which kids?' he cried. 'That's it, Marlena; I'm going up!'

'Don't,' I told him. 'Leave it, Paolo. Please.'

He looked at me, exasperated. From the floor above us came the sound of music; songs sung in a language I didn't know.

'That fucking radio!' Paolo snapped. 'That fucking woman!'

'She's alright,' I said. 'Leave her alone.'

'Don't be crazy, Marlena. You haven't a clue what you're saying.'

I had seen the mother of those kids, the woman upstairs. I saw her almost every day. Sometimes when I was out on the balcony she would come and string her laundry on the line above. I liked the way she moved. I could tell a lot about her, just by looking. I knew the exact way she would smile if I stepped aside to dodge the water dripping from her fresh-washed clothes. She wasn't Italian; her skin wasn't

Italian-brown. She was thin and black-haired – but not like any Sicilian woman I knew. Her eyes were different. They weren't stony or *borghesi* or full of dogma. I mean, she would stand up there with them shining; with her laundry pegs between her teeth and her arms stretched up to the line – and if the water hit my shoulders, she would laugh down at me as if the whole damned world was funny. As if she were waiting for me to laugh, too. I always did.

'What's her name?' I asked Paolo.

'Who?'

My eye had stopped bleeding now.

'The woman upstairs.'

Paolo shrugged.

'*Boh.*'

Boh. I couldn't stand the word. It kind of meant, 'I don't know and I can't be bothered to find out.' It was so lazy. Paolo said it all the time.

'I'd like to know,' I said.

'What?'

'Her name!' I started swaying to the radio. 'I like the way she moves. I think she is OK.'

'Will you stop that?' he said. 'You're not at work now! I don't care what her name is. I don't want anything to do with her. And I don't want you going near her either, do you hear? Her kids just assaulted you! Your eye is cut! They're different up there, Marlena. They're a different breed.'

I stood and stared at Paolo. Right then he felt far away. He was speaking; his mouth was moving – making word-shapes, opening and closing and showing his perfect teeth – but I couldn't really hear him. His voice was distant and slurred.

'A breed?' I repeated. 'Is that what you said?'

I felt like I was floating.

'Who, the Romanies?' I went on. 'The kids? Women? Tell me, who?'

Paolo answered, but I have no idea what he said. His image began to blur. My voice turned shallow; I tasted something on my tongue. Like the scent of flowers. Like an exotic perfume. Then everything changed colour, from white before my eyes to yellow to brown to black. I heard the chant: '*Bílá! Bílá!*' Then my legs buckled under me.

When you come round from unconsciousness, it's like swimming up from the darkest deep. There was this heaviness around me, pushing down upon my world. I remember wishing I could be rid of it. Then, like little gifts, my senses came back to me. Suddenly I could hear Paolo clearly. Next, my sight returned; I saw him above me, his light green eyes; his frantic curls. I could smell coffee; I tasted blood. And Paolo was talking.

'*Mi fanno schifo!*' he was saying. They disgust me. 'And I know what you're thinking! But I won't take it back! What I said about a breed! The fact is they're not like us, Marlena. They steal. They throw stones at girls! Savio says they build fires on their floors – in their houses, where they eat and sleep! *Madonna mia*, they'll end up killing us! They'll end up burning us to the ground!'

I inhaled. His bacon breath fell over my face.

'You're pathetic,' I told him as I tried to stand.

He offered his hand.

'Get out of my way.'

18

Her name was Dana. Once my eye had healed I went up to her flat. Not to talk to her about what had happened; I didn't care about that. I just wanted to see her, see where she lived. I don't know why; I guess I was looking for a friend.

As I climbed the steps the piss-smell got stronger. A couple of the boys who had thrown the stones were hanging down from the banister like apes. When they saw me they started, turning themselves right way up in a tangle of limbs.

'*Ciao*,' I called up to them as they shot out of sight.

Dana's door had been broken. There was a hole where the main lock had been. The wood around the hole was splintered and cracked. All the doors on our floor looked pretty strong; they had these brass nameplates screwed on to them too and vases at the side stuffed with silk lilies and leaves. But Dana's door had no vase or plate – and it was painted pale blue. There was a paper sun stuck above the letterbox with her surname – POUROVÁ – scrawled in crayon along one of the rays. It looked like a child had written it. With my fingers I traced the letters of the name. Then I knocked on the sun and I waited.

'*Ano?*' A woman's bright voice sounded behind the wood. '*Ano?*' it said again.

I stepped towards it.

'Hello,' I replied. 'I'm from downstairs. My name is Marlena. I've seen you sometimes – I think you've seen me?'

The door stayed shut; I came closer. I spoke through the little hole.

'I've seen you with your washing,' I said. 'I've just come up here, I mean, I've come to say hello.'

She opened the door and glowered at me. Then she flung her arms out in front of her body like a ringmaster and her scowl flipped to an insolent smile.

'Balcony Girl!' she cried.

Three tiny long-haired dogs with ribbons round their necks ran out from behind her legs, yapping.

'You're a stranger here too, eh? You have eyes like rockets firing off! *Com-e i raz-zi che si accen-dono. Si!*'

Her Italian was correct – but she spoke it jerkily, slow. The dogs fussed around my feet and licked my toes.

'Don't worry about them, the little rats.' She whispered behind her hand, as if they might understand. 'They don't bite even when you wish they would.'

Everywhere in Dana's flat was cheap crystal and white gold. There were shrines in all the alcoves, photographs, pictures of Jesus. Fake chandeliers hung from the ceiling with plastic candles and electric bulbs.

'You want coffee?' she asked me as I followed her down the hall, stepping over boxes and kids' toys. 'I make it Czech style, do you want some?'

'Sure,' I said. 'So you're Czech?'

'Half, yes. Half-Romany.'

'That's funny,' I said. 'I'm half-Italian.'

She giggled and imitated me: '*That's funny! Sure!*'

She breezed through into her kitchen and turned on the tap. It groaned and juddered as the water came out. I stood in the doorway. In a gentler voice she asked: 'You don't have a cigarette spare, no?'

I pulled out a pack of Dianas from my jeans and handed it to her open. She set a pan under the running water and took two. She lit one cigarette with a small, gold lighter she had on a chain around her neck. She blew smoke into the air. Then she brushed her hair to one side with lilac-painted fingernails, and slid the other behind her ear.

We drank from crystal glasses. Dana laid out biscuits on a plate. Her coffee was thick and sweet, gritty on my tongue. The Czechs don't filter it, they just chuck it all in a pan, boil it up and pour it straight. We went out on to the balcony and sat on stools. The evening sunlight made Dana's hair shine. Close up her face was gaunt and freckled and she had these fierce brown eyes. She wore gold around her wrists, her ankles, her toes and thumbs. She had on a white tracksuit that day; it made her skin look very dark. She laughed when she saw me looking. She said to me, ironic: 'I am a real gypsy woman, eh?'

And she ruffled my hair.

What I did then surprised me. I smiled up at her and I pushed my skull against her palm. Dana repeated her words – *I am a real gypsy woman* – and kept her hand upon my head as if I belonged to her. I gazed down over the railings on to the dirty road, and thought then of the times in England after my mother died – when I grew older, hard and rough, when I tagged strangers down the street, stealing from their pockets, when I set fire to the hedgerows and watched them burn. When I ran behind the sweet factory with the local boys, let them open my jeans and in the heartless dark explore me. When I threw stones.

We stayed out on the balcony until shadow covered the street. Then we went inside. In the back room of the flat the

TV was blaring cartoons. I walked through; in the corner an older girl was standing ironing clothes. She was beautiful. She had these huge, desolate eyes. Her brothers had come out of hiding now and were pushing each other around in front of the screen. When they saw me they stopped. The boy with the mole fixed his eyes upon me.

'What's your name?' I said.

'Kuba.'

He came towards me with a swagger; he smiled very bold. I held my hand out.

'I'm Marlena.'

To my surprise he shook it. When he did that the younger boy came and stood next to him.

'I'm Patrik!' he piped. 'You're the one who ran away!'

I lifted my hair and showed him my scar. His mouth and his eyes all made the same circle shape.

'I was scared,' I said. 'You hurt me.'

Kuba had to stop himself from laughing when I said that; I saw him pressing his lips together. I turned to the girl. She set the steaming iron upright on the board and lifted her head.

'And you?' I asked. 'What's your name?'

'She won't speak to you,' said Patrik. He turned to his brother. 'Will she?'

I looked at Kuba.

'Is she shy?'

He lowered his eyes, still smiling darkly. It was Patrik who exclaimed: 'She's scared, lady! She's scared of strangers, just like you!'

He stood on his tiptoes to whisper up. I stooped, felt his child's breath warm at my ear.

'*Dimmi*,' I told him.

'Her name is Anželika.'

*

Dana took a couple more cigarettes from me before I left. Then she asked me if Paolo's flat had hot water.

'Doesn't yours?' I asked.

She shook her head. We walked down the hall. As we said goodbye, I noticed a baseball bat propped up next to the door. The broken lock, a pile of old screws and a screwdriver lay on the floor.

'Trouble?' I said.

'Yes. Too much trouble here,' she replied.

Then Dana scratched her freckled nose and said, light-hearted as a bird: '*Ciao-ciao.*'

19

The next morning I awoke to the sound of knocking. I was surprised: no one ever called round in the daytime – unless they knew Paolo was in. He had left for university hours ago on the bike; I had watched him dress and pack his books in the shadows as I lay in bed. The knocking got louder. Whoever it was, they were already in the hall. I reached for Paolo's dressing gown and wrapped it around me. I put on my shoes.

Looking through the spyglass I saw four dark heads.

'Oh,' I said out loud.

It was Dana. I opened the door; Kuba and Patrik were standing in front of her on the welcome mat. At Dana's side, holding her hand tightly, was Anželika. The boys started giggling; they had towels and toothbrushes and shampoo bottles piled up in their arms. Dana leaned forward.

'Please, Marlena, can we take a shower?'

I paused. I was disorientated.

'It is just that you said you have hot water . . .'

'And you said you do not. What time is it?' I asked. Paolo wouldn't eat canteen dinners. He always came home for lunch.

'Gone twelve.'

'Can you be very quick?'

'Of course,' she said. 'Quick, quick.'

*

I swung the door open and they came inside. The layout of Paolo's flat was identical to their own; they knew where to go. They went ahead of me, and filed into the bathroom, leaving their shoes in a heap by the door. The boys had already begun to undress as they pushed their way in. They threw their clothes out in the hall and turned the lock behind them.

When they emerged the four were clean and bright. They had their hair slicked back from their faces.

'Come up later,' Dana said, as they left. 'I can tell your fortune.'

'You read tarot?' I asked.

'No.'

'What then? Palms? Crystal balls?'

Laughter erupted from her: 'Don't be silly!'

She wrapped her towel around her face like an old crone's headscarf and made her hands into two dramatic claws. Then she flashed her eyes at me, announcing: 'I read tea!'

I blushed. There was something about Dana's playfulness; about the way she looked at me as she climbed the stairs with her three clean kids. Her wet hair fell straggling down her back, darkening her clothes; her eyes then were mellow, warm. All at once, for no reason, I wanted to tell her to stay with me.

'Tea?' I repeated.

I could barely hear my own voice. She slung the towel over her shoulder and was gone.

That evening we drank from bone china rimmed with gold. Dana stared matter-of-factly at the black patches of tea-leaves washed up on one side of my cup and said: 'It doesn't suit you, what you are doing here. Your feet are itching; you're not in love. You must leave here. You are bored, Rocket Girl! It's so easy to see it. You are not close to your destiny in Catania.'

'Where will I go?' I asked.

She shrugged. 'I don't know.'

'But can you see anyone else? Another man?'

'I can see *something*,' she said. 'I can see blood!'

I started to laugh.

'Give me a break.'

But she didn't think it was funny. She put the cup down, placing her hands upon her knees. Then she raised those hands to my shoulders and pushed down hard on to my bones.

When I got back to the flat, Paolo was in. I didn't want to speak to him; I went straight to the bathroom. The faint smell of Dana – of her kids – was still in the air. I had to get ready – I had a shift to work at Mickeys.

'Where have you been?' he shouted through. He was in the kitchen, fiddling with the TV.

'Upstairs,' I shouted back. 'I've been talking to Dana.'

Paolo came to the bathroom door with his hands on his hips like a woman.

'*What?*' I said. 'What the fuck do you want?'

'I don't want you to go there! I don't know *why* you go there! I don't understand you Marlena. You have everything you need here.'

'Oh? I go there because I like her, Paolo. I don't know anyone else in Catania apart from you and Savio and a load of club strippers. And you don't want me hanging around with them either, do you?'

I took my shirt off and hung it on the rail.

'I think you need to listen to me,' he said.

'And I think I need to move out of here. I can't breathe around you!'

He folded his arms. His eyes filled up with stupid tears. I turned my back to him, ran a sink full of steaming water and took off my bra.

I thought Paolo would leave then – return to the TV in silence and brood – but he didn't. Instead he came up behind me and began to kiss my back in a way he had never done before.

'Don't,' I said. 'I have to work.'

'Please,' he whispered.

'Don't,' I said, again.

But he pushed his hands up my skirt. He found my sex and persisted with his fingers until I was wet. Then he undid his belt; I heard his trousers fall around his feet. I don't know why I let him do it – but anyway what did it matter? It was over in a heartbeat. And it was for the last time.

It was just like Dana said: I wasn't in love; I was bored. I was bored of Paolo, of his ways and his views; I was bored as he moved inside me. The ventilator on the wall was humming; I listened to it turn. Paolo's grip on me grew tighter. I heard him moaning at my back. I counted the times he said my name, his grunts, his whimpers, his shallow breath. Then he was sobbing at my back and his whole body was trembling, and I felt nothing.

When he moved, I washed between my legs. I pulled down my skirt. I sat on the bath-side and put on black stockings.

'Don't move out,' he pleaded, watching me. 'You can't move out. I love you.'

His voice was weak, like a man who tells lies. I buttoned my shirt. I breathed in and out in the steam and the hum, waiting for him to go.

20

I went up to Dana's most days. I went just to be with her, to get away from Paolo. He still didn't get why I wanted to go there. The thought of Dana and I together – I think it scared him. He kept harping on about the other things I could do with my days; he could find me work, he said. He talked about me cleaning somewhere or washing up in a kitchen. And maybe I would have done it if he hadn't been so insistent. I was getting tired of Mickeys: the girls, the guys, the broken faces – and it was so far out. From Via Soreca, Mickeys was a long, lonely haul across town.

Up at Dana's I could sit for hours on the balcony, watching the trains rumble north, to Messina or south, to Siracusa. I would see the passengers gazing out of the carriages; sometimes I would wave back at the kids who waved at me. In March, white olive blossom fell and covered the tracks. In April came rains with electric skies. Kuba and Patrik were always out in the tenement garden, fighting and digging and wrecking the fence. If Anželika came out with them she just used to stand like a ghost under the trees. She had a face that was spooked all right; I wondered what was wrong with her. She never smiled – and she didn't move the way you expect a child to move either: she didn't jump around or dance or take up space. Anželika. She just used to stand and stare. It was like she was trying her best to disappear.

One night after the kids had gone to bed, Dana took a bottle of *slivovice* from the cabinet. It was some awful Moravian drink; Dana called it Devil's Piss. We drank it neat and warm. It went straight to my head. We played cards for a while. Dana taught me how to play *žolík*. We put on hats. I took a veil Dana had made out of coarse black lace and hung it over my face; she wore a white fedora. Then she went through to the bedroom and returned wearing a smart red coat with big brass buttons up the middle and a white collar of real rabbit fur.

'What do you think?' she asked.

'You look like a spy!'

'I stole this coat,' she told me. 'Years ago, from some old *signora*. I was selling roses door-to-door. I had a big, black bucket of flowers. Anyway I went in this swanky café – you know the Rialta, on Via Stromboli? – and I asked this poor bastard if he wanted to buy one, buy a stupid rose, *rozumíš*? But his wife – Marlena, you wouldn't believe it! – she slapped his hand as he took out the money – ha, ha! She actually did that! She slapped his hand! She said she wouldn't buy from a gypsy. She told him I was dirty! So I swiped the coat to serve her right, from the back of her chair, just like that. Ha, ha, ha! I took it from right under her nose! She didn't notice a thing, the old witch. She was too busy making her face as long as a horse!'

Dana turned up the coat collar victoriously then pranced from side to side, thrusting her hands into the pockets. When she pulled them out again, she suddenly looked serious. She took off her hat and shook down her hair.

'I suppose you take a lot of shit out at Mickeys,' she said, walking across the room and collapsing into a chair. 'Anyone ever get rough with you?'

'Not yet,' I replied. 'Not there. At least, nothing that bad.'

'Then you are lucky,' she said, fixing her eyes on me.

She let her hands fall into her lap. We faced each other now, and I eyed the red coat.

'Thief,' I called her.

'Slut,' she whispered back.

By the time I left the flat I was too drunk to speak. Dana walked with me down the hall. We stood at the door and, before she opened it, she put her arms around me and sighed.

'You are a good girl,' she said. 'You are a good girl and I like you.'

She was unsteady on her feet; she kept closing her eyes. I put my arms out too, rubbed my cheek upon her cheek. I could smell her hair, musky and sweet; feel the brass buttons of her coat press into my belly and breasts. We held each other tight then, like sisters.

21

A few days later I was on my own at Via Soreca, sewing. I had ripped my rose dress the night before at Dana's. I don't know exactly how it happened; we were drunk again. Anyway, I wasn't having much luck; it was cold in the flat. My fingers couldn't work the needle. I decided to make tea to warm up my hands.

When I went to the kitchen there was no sugar. I stared into the empty bowl. Tea without sugar makes me spit. I decided to go and borrow some from Dana. Maybe she would talk to me for a while. I left my dress and black thread on the bed and took up a cup.

I knocked twice on the door. There was no answer. I turned to leave, thinking I would come back later – but then I changed my mind and just for the hell of it I knocked on the door one more time.

'*Ano?*'

The voice was not Dana's. It was soft, servile.

'Anželika?'

'Marlena?'

'Yes, it's me.'

'Minute. Wait. Dana market. Minute, please.'

I heard a sound like wood scraping along the floor. Then the hall light came on and I saw Anželika's face appear behind the glass panel above the apartment door.

'*Ciao,*' I said. 'What's up?'

She pressed her face against the glass. I stood back and lifted up my cup.

'Can I have some of your sugar?' I asked.

Then I tried it again in her language, from the scraps of Czech I had learned from Dana's endless offers of coffee and tea.

'*Cukr? Maš cukr?*'

I wasn't sure she would understand – but Anželika's face vanished and I heard the scraping sound again. She must have been standing on a chair. I thought it had been a game for me; I waited for her to open the door. But she didn't; instead, she pushed a skinny brown hand through the letterbox and beckoned towards the cup with two of her fingers. I gave it to her. She went away without saying anything, and a short time later the hand came through the box again. This time the cup was full.

'Thank you,' I said to her.

Then I leaned down and put my mouth up to the lock hole.

'Thank you,' I said again.

Anželika's voice when she replied still haunts me: 'No problem. Thank *you*, Marlena friend. Thank *you*.'

I went back to mending my dress. But with each stitch I thought about what had happened. Someone locked in a room means something is fucked up. I kept hearing Anželika's words in my head. She wasn't in danger up there; I could tell that from her face – but something was wrong. Maybe she was in some bad trouble with Dana.

With the final stitches of my dress I pricked my thumb. I watched a dark ball of blood well up on my skin. I sucked at it; the ball came back. What if she needed to get out? What if there was a fire?

I decided to ask Dana about it when she got back. In the meantime I went through to the kitchen and ran cold water over my thumb. From the sink I looked out of the window and down into the garden. Then I made more tea, and sweetened it.

22

'Dana?'

She was back from town. The dogs were barking like crazy. She opened the door and kissed me.

'Can I come in?'

'Can you come *in*? What do you mean? Of course! *Marlenko!*'

'I wanted to ask you something,' I said. I stepped into the hall. We stood opposite each other behind the door now, beside the broken lock and screws. 'I came up earlier, Dana. I saw Anželika.'

'She told me. You came to take sugar. You want tea? Or coffee?' She walked through to the kitchen.

'Okay.' I followed her and sat down.

'She had to pass it through the letterbox,' I told her. 'She was locked in.'

'Yes. I know.'

'Why do you do that?'

'What do you mean why do I do it? Why are you asking me all these questions? Have you come here to interrogate me? What business is it of yours?'

I wondered if I should go. 'I'm sorry,' I told her. 'I don't mean any harm.'

Her eyes flashed at me.

'I was thinking of Anželika. Her being locked up. That's all.'

'Well don't,' she snapped. 'And give me a cigarette, can you?'

I did. I watched her light it. Her hands were shaking. She took sharp, quick puffs.

'What's wrong?'

She disappeared down the hall muttering to herself and when she came back she had the baseball bat in her hands.

'You see this?' she said. 'We had a guest! You know my broken door, my broken chain? We had a guest – in a mask! You see how my life is, Marlena?'

I reached out to her; she edged away. 'What did he do to you?'

'What do you think?'

'Were you on your own here? What about the kids?'

'The boys were out. They were on the tracks. I could hear them! I could hear them through the window! Singing 'Scalinatella'! As he took my money. As he made me undress – and – '

She couldn't say the word. She took another of my cigarettes and stared bitterly at the floor. I smoked too. Our shoulders touched. We stayed like that, standing in her kitchen, for what seemed a long time.

'Where was Anželika?' I asked, when I finally spoke.

'She was here.'

A bad taste filled my mouth.

'She was with me. We were making *knedliky*. We had the radio on, we were singing along, being stupid. He split the lock and walked right in, I never heard a thing.'

Dana threw me a black look then put her head in her hands: 'I never heard a fucking thing.'

My stomach began to hurt. Dana barked a string of words in Czech and Anželika came through. She stood in front of her mother and I and, when Dana nodded, she lifted up her skirt. I swallowed. A mass of scars covered her thin brown thighs. I leaned forward and looked closer; I touched the hard lumps of tissue one after another as Dana began to cry. Most of the scars were quick knife slashes, messy stab wounds, little cuts – but the ones nearest her sex were words carved into the flesh.

BOTTANA RUMENA was what they said.

Gypsy whore.

23

Getting out of Catania was easy for me. I make the big decisions quick. I took my stuff; I called Mickeys and quit. I'm always leaving places. I like the way it makes me feel.

By the time I got back down to Paolo's, Savio was there. I don't know how long he had been hanging around – but he was drunk and so was Paolo; there were empty bottles all over the table and the TV was on.

'Hello, darling!' said Savio. 'We were wondering where you had been!'

'Upstairs,' I replied.

'Oh?' said Paolo.

I was breathless, dazed.

'Yeah. I've been talking to Dana. Paolo, did you know there was an attack? Were you around when it happened – last summer? Was anyone else here about?'

'*Boh*,' he said. 'Who cares? Last summer was ages ago.'

'Those gypsies are always killing each other!' Savio laughed. 'What was it this time – a *crime passionnel*?'

'No.'

'An attack upstairs?' said Paolo. 'That sounds a bit crazy, Marlena. I've told you, they're a different kind. I don't know why you listen to her. She just wants money. It'll be some sob story for a handout. She's probably just making it up.'

I glared at him, but he wasn't looking. A woman on the TV had bent over a fridge to open the salad shelf. The show host was honking a black rubber horn in his hand as the camera zoomed up between her legs. Savio slapped his hand down on the table and shrieked. Paolo started sniggering too. Pretty soon they were holding their bellies with laughter.

'Hey, Marlena!' Savio shouted as I walked through into the bedroom. 'I see you've been mending your little dress. Why don't you put it on – you're so damned pretty! Put it on for Paolo – and for me!'

I closed the bedroom door. I moved quickly. The TV and the voices became a single drone; I let them drift away. I pulled down my suitcase from the wardrobe top and placed the rose dress in it, the pins, the cotton and the needle. One by one I threw in the rest of my things. Then I scribbled Dana a note to slide under her door.

'AM GOING', it read. 'SEE YOU IN TIME? MARLENA.'

Looking in my purse I took out the taxi card the guy Arnaldo had handed me on the night I arrived in Sicily. I began to call the number. Savio and Paolo were still laughing to themselves, oblivious, as I crept down the hall and let the door to 315 Via Soreca swing shut behind me.

24

Arnaldo took me north and didn't ask me for a fare. He didn't ask questions either. He was just the same as he had been on my first night in Catania, sweating and ranting and driving like he was in a getaway. He smoked one cigarette after another. Almost as soon as I got into his cab he was cursing the state: Feo, Lamorte, *Viva l'Italia*. He pointed to vandalized tenements, broken windows and graffitied walls which read EAT THE RICH and CANDY CANDY I LOVE YOU I NEED YOU. We drove out of the city and that felt good.

Once we hit the coast road I leaned out of my window. The sky was orange; the sea silver. With those colours, Arnaldo's radio playing songs and the sun pushing up into the morning I felt suddenly excited, new. I looked out over the Mediterranean, saw the boats returning from the dawn catch with their front lamps shining. I could smell fish on the air; diesel and wet salt. Arnaldo smiled at me as we took on the rise and the black crags of the northern coast appeared.

It turned out he lived in Calatabiano – a small, grey town a few kilometres south of Taormina.

'My hometown,' he said, as we passed the signs and slowed down. 'Now, where do you want to go? Further north? To Taormina? Messina?'

'I don't know,' I told him. 'Take me anywhere.'

He looked at me and frowned; he was confused.

'I'm sorry, Arnaldo. It's just that things are all fucked up and I don't really know where I'm going.'

'Okay,' he said. 'Leave it to me.'

He took me to his flat.

'It isn't much,' he said, as he turned the taxi into a yard full of junk.

An old washing machine stood in one corner; set into the other was a corrugated door. We got out and I heard voices; the door was opened just enough for me to see the eyes and black hair of a woman. Lower down, around her knees, the face of a small boy poked out. He gazed at me for a second, then hid his face in his mother's skirts. But when he heard Arnaldo calling his name – *Ismael, Ismael, cos'hai fatto tutt'il giorno?* – he ran to him and yelled out in delight.

Arnaldo's wife wasn't Sicilian; she was too dark. She had the skin and lips of an African woman – and large jet eyes. As she pulled the iron door towards her I watched her dress-strap slip from her shoulder to show the top of a full, brown breast. Arnaldo quickstepped over the threshold and pushed it gently back.

'Fatima,' he said, introducing us one to the other. 'This is Marlena. Marlena – Fatima. She is from Algiers. She is my wife.'

He turned to her and to my surprise he said a few words in Arabic; I don't know what. Maybe he was explaining what I was doing there on her doorstep. But if I closed my eyes, I couldn't tell it was Arnaldo speaking; that I was there with an Italian man. As he spoke so naturally, Fatima began to nod and smile. Then Arnaldo asked me to come inside.

The two of them lived with the boy in a single room. On one side of it was a kitchen and a metal toilet behind a board. In the middle of the room stood a table. Over the other side was a wide brass bed; by the bed was a net curtain. At first I thought it was covering a wall-cupboard, but then Arnaldo walked over to it.

'This is where you'll sleep tonight,' he said, pulling the net back to reveal a small bed.

A few coloured blankets lay on a thin mattress; there was a pile of toys on the floor. There wasn't room for anything else in there. The bed filled up the whole space.

'Usually it is for my son,' Arnaldo said.

I looked in and picked up a toy horse from the pillow; it squeaked when I squeezed it.

'Usually?'

'Tonight it is for you.'

I put the squeaking horse down again.

'Thanks,' I said.

We stepped back and Arnaldo let the curtain fall.

That night, Fatima cooked. I sliced tomatoes for her. Arnaldo reached underneath the bed and brought out a big green bottle of wine.

'*Vino di campagna!*' he exclaimed. 'I buy it on the hill.'

'So you drink?' I asked Fatima as she nudged him to fill up her glass.

'Only a little,' she smiled. 'And only in private!'

'Are you Moslem?' I asked her.

'Yes. And I love Allah. It's just that sometimes,' she said, beginning to giggle and turning her brimming gaze to Arnaldo: 'Well, yes, sometimes I forget him.'

We all forgot Allah that night. We played cards until late. The hours went by.

'So, will you look for new work?' Arnaldo asked me as I stood up to go to bed.

'I'll have to, I guess.'

'I think they want workers on the hill,' he said. 'Fatima, do you remember what Giosetta said?'

'Whereabouts on the hill?'

'Near Motta Camastra, where I get the wine.'

'Is it farm work?' I asked.

'Not really. More reconstruction.'

I stayed silent and watched Arnaldo's burgundy-stained lips as they moved to tell me: 'Schigghiapeddi is the name you should ask for. They're gutting the old farm, rebuilding it. I know the draughtsman; he's one of the sons. He studied architecture I think – he packed it in or something, couldn't stand the bullshit. But he knows what he's doing all right. He's good.'

'What is his name?' I whispered, although I knew what he would say.

Arnaldo smiled for a second.

'His name is Jula.'

Fatima lifted the boy Ismael out of the cupboard-bed and placed him in the brass one. Then she pulled back the blankets from the mattress and took away the squeaking horse.

'Please,' she gestured. 'Sleep.'

I took off my shoes and lay down. I was too tall to fit. I turned on my side and curled my knees to my stomach like a baby in a womb.

'Goodnight,' Fatima whispered. '*Layla zaida*.'

'*Layla zaida*,' I replied.

Happy dreams. She looked very beautiful as she turned out the light.

I couldn't sleep in the cupboard-bed. My head was spinning with wine; I couldn't stop thinking. Maybe I got a few hours' rest, I don't know: strange images filled my night. I dreamed of walking down roads that were grey and endless. I dreamed I had nowhere to go. When I awoke at seven I couldn't tell if I had slept. I awoke to a pushing sound. I heard a whimper. Then the scrape of metal upon wood.

Through the curtain, I saw the boy Ismael circling a toy car around on the floor. Behind him was Fatima's shape. She was making little noises. She was rocking her body back and forth upon the bed. Arnaldo had his arms outstretched and was saying her name, cupping her breasts with his hands as she moved towards him and away. Each time she pushed back, her body-sound deepened; then almost against her will she let out a cry. I heard a flood of words as she began to kiss Arnaldo and bury her face in his hair. The whole time, the boy had been playing with the car, just circling.

I decided I would leave after breakfast. I would go and find Jula. I pulled the blankets up over my shoulders and glanced around the room. Drunk and stumbling in the darkness, I hadn't noticed the walls the night before. In the light of new morning I saw they were covered with pictures and paper shapes. From the ceiling small shells hung down on strings. Soothed by the laughter now of my hosts, I fell asleep. And I slept deeply this time, dreamed I was a fisherman, a fish; a rock being shaped by the sea.

TWO

B*ack on the mainland I carry a photograph in my pocket. It is in black and white. It is of Jula. I took it myself one night at the farm. I held Jula's old Nikon up in front of his face and dared to watch him. I was clumsy with the camera, nervous; I remember I could barely manage a simple snapshot. My time in Sicily was running out and I knew it. By then it was late June.*

In the frame Jula is not alone. He is with Paolo and Savio. They are drinking and playing cards. They are playing poker at a table. There is a little girl there too: she is thick-haired and thin. No-one else can see her except me; she is crouched under an empty chair. She is eating a raw carrot and squatting in the dust, shouting – Marlena, per favore, non mi piacciono le fotografie! – that she does not like to be in pictures.

The card table is outside in the shade of a cedar tree. There is a pile of money on it – crumpled notes, a few coins: over three hundred thousand lire. Paolo and Savio sit grim-faced, their mouths downturned, their eyes studying their hidden hands. This is the last chance to take the jackpot. This is the final game.

I, of course, am no longer in the round. My cards, worth nothing, lie face down under my glass. But Jula holds his lot calmly, close; he guards a royal flush. Safe in this knowledge, he forgets the game for a second and stares into the lens.

Desire runs like voltage through my body. My fingers twist him into focus. When I see his image there sharp my legs begin to shake; I feel my blood pulse down between them. He knows, and looks longer, deeper. I think I see him smile. I can't stand it and I can't wait so I press down hard and the shutter drops black. He is swallowed up with the dying light and it is over.

Jula lowers his eyes. He pours another vodka and flips his hand: I see a red ten, jack, ace; the king and queen of hearts. He grins at Paolo – then he turns to Savio, who is cursing him now, calling him gypsy trash.

'You filthy bastard!' Savio is screaming. 'What was she doing over there? With the camera, eh? You've screwed us over – she was making signs! You little mongrel – you've stitched us up!'

Savio is very angry. I want to take his picture. I want to look into his face and laugh. But by now I know that he is dangerous – so I sit down and keep still as he shifts and twitches. I watch the words flare bitterly from his mouth.

'You're crazy,' Jula tells him.

'I had nothing to do with it,' is all I say.

I put the cap back on the camera lens and Jula pulls the prize towards him.

I

I left Arnaldo's around nine. He and Fatima were sleeping. I took some bread from their kitchen and left them a note. Then I walked out into the yard where the boy Ismael was sitting on a box in the sunlight.

'Which way is Motta Camastra?' I asked.

He pointed right.

It was a Sunday morning, still too early for church. The streets were empty, cool; as I walked heat filled them. My head got sore after a while; my skin began to shine. I stopped at a bar called *Luna Rossa*. I pushed my head through a set of rainbow-coloured door blinds and saw a boy standing cleaning glasses with a rag.

'Are you open?' I asked.

'*Vuole mangiare?*'

'I just want a glass of water. And a coffee. A black one.'

'Black coffee for the white girl,' he replied.

I sat down at the bar and pushed three coins towards him.

I asked the boy how I could get to Motta Camastra. He said on Sundays there was no way. I asked him how long it would take me to walk. He laughed and glanced down at my case.

'With that? With the sun already up? What do you want there anyway? It's not a tourist town. It's not even a town. Just a few farms, a few crazies. A heap of fruit trees. Nothing.'

'I'm looking for Jula Schigghiapeddi,' I told him.

A breeze blew through the blinds and made them flutter. The boy laid his hands flat upon the bar top and exhaled, echoing the wind.

That boy, he couldn't have been more than sixteen. His skin was covered in black down. His expression was a funny one: he looked wise and innocent all at once, young and old. I waited beneath the sound of Jula's name as he slung his glass-cloth over his shoulder and picked up the phone. Then once the call was over, he said in a low, courteous voice that I should finish my drink and go with him, if it was not too much trouble.

No, I replied, it was not.

So we walked back through the blinds into the glare of the street. He carried my case; he put a hand at the small of my back. We crossed the road; we went down a back-street and over a metal bridge. On the other side we stuck to the river path. Through the trees, rays of green-gold sun played on my face and on the boy's black hair.

'You need to ask in here,' he told me as a long, white building came into view.

It was on the water's edge. It had steps leading up to it and windows in black, plate glass.

'It's Jula's sister you want,' he said to me. 'Analisa.'

He turned back along the path and raised his hand in the flickering light.

'What is this place?' I called to him.

'Nina's? Why, it's the Casino.'

2

Nina's was the saddest place I ever saw. After that day spent looking for Analisa I never went there again. Glazed-eyed women stood at one-armed bandits, pulling the levers over and over; old men hung around in corners, offering their cigarettes to angel-faced boys. They were a weird crowd: different from the regulars you got in Mickeys. They wore expensive stuff, furs and frills and gold – but they looked so cheap and poor. They looked dirty, the crowd in Nina's. They all looked like ghouls.

As I walked along the arcades a woman in a mink threw me a look. I stopped and faced her just in case she was Analisa.

'Yough waghnt something?' she said, gargling her Italian vowels in the back of her throat like she was choking.

'No,' I replied.

'Then geght ought of my light!'

From the way she spoke I knew she was German, maybe Austrian. I looked at her navy seamed stockings, her rings, her tangled hair. She turned back to her game and three red cherry bunches came rolling up in the machine window.

'Did yough heaghr what I saighd?'

The bunches went clack-clack-clack.

'It's okay,' I said. 'It's not you I'm looking for.'

*

Past the arcades was a huge gaming area. I didn't stop in there. Instead I made my way through the crowds of gamblers to a door at the back of the hall. When I got to it I pushed it; it opened on to a small room filled with smoke. There were men in the room, but no cards or croupiers, no machines or roulette wheels; just a few battered tables and the smell of male sweat. Stepping inside I thought for a second I was the only woman there. I turned to leave. Then I spotted a couple of girls in the corner. I walked over.

As I got closer the girl nearest to me looked up and started to laugh. She was black-skinned, yellow-haired; she was scrawny and young. She wore no top, only a green-sequinned skirt; her nipples were pierced with big gold hoops.

'Go, Kiki!' someone shouted to her.

She bent over a tabletop, snorted a line of coke with a banknote.

'Go, Kiki, go!'

The other girl was older. She was standing at the blinds. She had her back turned to the crowd. Thick, red hair fell in waves down her body.

'Analisa?'

She swung around and gave me an artless smile. She was tall, beautiful – but she had heroin eyes. Suddenly I didn't want to look at her. I fixed my eyes on the tartan floor.

'*Si?*' she replied.

I lifted my head.

'I've heard there's work at your farm up on Etna. Working for Giosetta?'

'That's my mother,' she told me. 'Sorry. She only takes men.'

'I can do a man's job.'

'That doesn't matter. She hates women. Who are you anyway? She won't accept.'

I was about to tell her my name when a fat man leaned forward from his table, tipping his chair. He was bald; he had moles all over his face. He grabbed Analisa by the hips and pulled her on to his knee.

'There's plenty of work for women here!' he chortled. He shoved his chubby hands under her vest and pulled at her breasts. 'Come on', he whispered in her ear. 'I've got places to be.'

'I want to go to the farm,' I interrupted. 'I don't care if your mother says no. I want to go there and I want you to take me. My name is Marlena Lupone. I want to see your brother, Jula.'

Something changed in Analisa then. Some kind of light flashed in her eyeholes.

'Can you wait?' she asked.

'Yes.'

She went down some stairs with the bald man and came back twenty minutes later with a handful of notes. Then she made a call from a little silver mobile with a blue fluorescent light.

'Franco, it's me.'

It was all she said.

Things moved fast after that. Analisa tied her hair back, picked up her jacket and lit a cigarette.

'Come with me,' she mouthed, doubling back down the stairs.

She went through a fire exit – and I was outside again, under the gold and the green of the trees. She walked quickly; with my case, I trailed behind. She turned a corner into a car park and got into a white pickup truck. She swung the passenger door open. I climbed in. The truck stank of grass. The floor was strewn with dead matches; the dashboard covered in chocolate wrappers, dust. Analisa started the engine.

As she drove, she grew tense – like there was no time. Whenever we stopped – at junctions, crossroads, lights – she shouted '*Come on! Come on!*' and drummed her fingers on the wheel. I saw her hands were grubby then; she had blisters on her palms. Underneath chipped pink varnish her nails were warped and brown. She slammed her fist down on the horn if we had to stop for too long; she wound down her window and yelled '*Fanculo!*' to the cars in front – and when she did that I knew we were getting closer; because the air poured in all around us, thick and warm and sweet and just like Jula had described it on that first night in the club: air with a honey-smell.

Analisa stopped only once on our way there. She pulled in under a railway bridge a few kilometres from the farm. We were deep in the country now: there were no cars or people, no houses around. When she turned the key and the engine fell silent, all I could hear was her finger-drumming, the rustling of her jacket; the sharp edges of her breath. She scratched her face. She smoked a couple of cigarettes. She turned the radio on and then off again. She had just started to dial a number into her mobile when we heard a sound; she looked up like a dog on guard. It was a bike, a motorbike. It was coming up behind us.

Analisa leaned out of the truck window. She glanced at me, excited for a moment, her face igniting like a breaking circuit.

'*Ciao, Francito!*' she hollered. 'I thought I had missed you!'

The guy Franco jumped off his bike and walked over. When he reached the truck he squatted down at window-height. He was short, square-faced; he looked in with pellet eyes. I had seen him someplace before.

'Hello, sister,' he said.

He dropped three small cellophane bags into Analisa's

hand. She reached into her coat and gave him her cash. He counted it swiftly then asked me: 'You want some? You looking to score?'

I counted the seconds between his question and my answer: 'No.'

He shrugged and stood up. He got back on the bike. As he tilted his head to put on his helmet I remembered how I knew him. He had a birthmark on the top of his crown. He was one of the guys I had seen hanging around below Paolo's flat on the night of the storm. The night of the Mercedes, the guys moving boxes. I was sure it was him; that mark like a heart. He revved up his bike and was gone; Analisa turned the radio on again.

'It's going to be a good day!' she giggled. 'Don't you think?'

And she started to sing along. *If you really love me, love me truly, Yeah Yeah Yeah.*

As we drove further up into the hills the lanes became narrower, banked by drystone walls and prickling grass. I reached out and touched the grass-heads, thinking of what I had said to Franco. No, I wasn't looking to score. Mount Etna filled the horizon now – massive, smoking, capped with snow. I looked behind me, saw the long, straight road, the sky, the dull green line of the sea. We slowed down and turned a final corner. Morning glory bloomed bright blue in the hedgerows; on our left a pine forest began.

'That's the farm,' Analisa said, pointing upwards and to her right as a dark building with double arches loomed into view.

She dropped down a gear and swung the pickup on to a black dirt track which was broken in places, rough – and strewn with the last of April's mandarins.

3

'**N**o.'
  Giosetta Schigghiapeddi shook her head and pursed her lips so tight that dozens of tiny lines crowded round her mouth, betraying her age.

'No, no. Absolutely, no. What would I do with you here? We have no need for a girl.'

'I'm strong,' I said.

'I don't care if you're an ox, *carina*! Girls cause trouble. They make men weak! Now take your suitcase and go back down the hill.'

She started to cough; she sounded like an old man. She doubled up and spat a ball of phlegm into the grass. Then she turned her back to me and grumbled at Analisa:

'*Malaccorta! Disadattata!* What in God's name were you thinking?'

Analisa wasn't listening. She was searching in her jacket for Franco's gear. She looked at her mother blankly.

'*Boh*,' she said.

I watched as the pair of them walked off in different directions. Giosetta climbed on to the scrub banks and stared out at the sea. Analisa hurried towards the farm. As she reached the veranda, a little girl ran from inside the house. She was dark-haired and young – maybe four or five. She leapt down the steps when she saw Analisa and clung to her leg.

'*Mamma, mamma!*' she cried. 'I found you something today; I picked clover, come and see!'

'Wait for me a while, Lola. I'll be down.'

'No you won't!' the child squealed.

Analisa kept walking. She disappeared through a side door. The girl stamped a bare foot on the ground. Then she looked up to the banks and saw Giosetta.

'*Nonna!*' she shouted. '*Nonna!*'

But Giosetta didn't come. It was just me and the child. I looked at her and she started to cry.

'Please don't,' I said.

She slumped on to the step and started sifting dust with her hands.

'I'll cry when I want,' she replied – still sifting, until her palms and fingers and tiny nails had turned deep brown with the dirt, almost black.

I stayed with Lola then. From where we sat on the step we could see for miles. 'So where's your *papà*?' I asked.

'He's dead. He made himself a pear.'

'What?'

'He made himself a pear!'

'I'm sorry,' I told her. 'A pear? I don't understand.'

She was using phrases I didn't know; sometimes she spoke in dialect. She scrunched up her face and squinted, pointing to a patch of blackish land in the far distance, beyond the lanes.

'Out there, he did it. Over there, in the woods. My Uncle Savio says he'd been dead for days, he says he had it coming. He had a needle in his arm and his body was blue and you know there's nothing you can do with that kind of a man, there's no way you can save a junkie.'

'And that's what you call it when someone does that? *Farsi una pera*?'

'Yeah. *Farsi una pera*. Where are you from anyway, *signorina*? Everyone around here knows that.'

'I'm from England. Mind if I stay with you a while, before I go?'

'I don't mind. Can I look at your things?'

So I closed my eyes and sat with the arches at my back, half in shadow, half in sun, as Lola sprung the brass catch of my case and rummaged through my clothes.

4

It was the sound of a violin. It was a Bach sonata. It was naked, sheer; it came from somewhere at the top of the house. I turned my head slowly and opened my eyes. Suddenly the world looked sharp-edged and clean.

'You were sleeping,' Lola said.

'I was dreaming,' I answered. 'I was dreaming I could hear music.'

I looked at her. She was wearing my white bowler hat. I said: 'You look pretty like that.'

'It's my uncle,' she replied. She started clicking her jaw.

'Playing the fiddle? Your uncle Jula?'

She nodded. Then she began conducting in the air with two dirty fingers.

'My grandmother says I have the wrong bones to be beautiful,' she told me, tipping the bowler over her eyes. Then she asked: 'Want to go see him?'

She stood up and so did I.

'Yes.'

Lola led me up the steps and through the stone arches. They divided the main building; they formed a tunnel between the front of the farm and the back. Underneath them it was dark and damp. Buckets and boxes were stacked up there. There was a makeshift kitchen and a big blue canister of gas. We went through a door in the right arch wall.

We passed through hazy rooms filled with rubble and wood. Then Lola opened a second door and brightness hit me. She smiled as I covered my eyes. She took me up a flight of new stairs, clearing them two at a time, jumping over piles of shavings, tools, ends of wood. I held on to the banister – it was carved with flowers – and breathed in the smell of planed pine.

We walked down a corridor. The music grew louder. We passed tubs full of plaster, towers of bricks and books. Then we climbed a few more stairs and reached another hall.

'The top room!' Lola announced.

The light up there made my eyes smart. Lola began to run. She yelled:

'*Zio, zio!* There's a lady from England! Look at me, *zio Jula!* Look at me in her hat!'

The sonata swelled around us now. Lola sprang into the doorway and bowed. The music faltered, then stopped; I heard a man's laugh. Without the sound of the violin the air seemed to vibrate. Lola back-stepped into the hallway and motioned with her hand. I walked in behind her, into the glare. I was dazzled. I felt like I hadn't woken up, like I was still on the edge of my dream. We were in a large, white-painted room.

Terracotta tiles covered the floor. In the corner was a low, white bed. There was a mirror at one wall and I saw myself in it. Then – suddenly – Jula, wiping his brow with his arm and turning around. He caught my eye in the reflection of the glass. He was nothing like I remembered from the club. He looked quiet, cautious. His hands were big and clean. He put down his instrument, his cheeks flushing the colour of young wine; I placed my suitcase on the floor. He had this way of looking at me – like he had known me across lifetimes.

'Hello,' he said, as if he had been expecting me. 'Hello, Marlena.'

'She wants a job here and *nonna* won't let her!' Lola cried.

She started jumping up and down on the bed.

'Why does she always say no to everything, *zio*? What's wrong with everybody here? And when will you mend my tricycle? When will you come and play?'

Jula took her soil-stained hands and clasped them.

'I'll talk to *nonna*,' he told her. 'Then I'll fix the bike.'

5

B y noon it was settled: I had a job.

'You can stay,' Jula told me as he walked on to the veranda.

The sun hung in a fury above us.

'She agreed to it?'

He came and leaned on the balcony rail.

'Not exactly,' he said. 'But she thinks I'll leave her. She says I'm her only reminder of happiness. Imagine that! Six weeks she spent with my father. Then he disappeared – never wrote, called. She loved him and he left her. That was it. That's why she asked me to do the plans in the first place – to keep me here. I have his face. I have his way, she says. I hate it, Marlena. It weighs on me. It's like I'm carrying round a dead man, trying to make him come alive.'

'I lied to her,' I told him. 'I can't do builders' work. I'm a dancing waitress! I don't know what use I'll be.'

'It doesn't matter about that. I could do it all myself. To tell you the truth I'm just sick of being here alone.'

'It's lonely?'

'It's fucked up is what it is.'

'It can't be more fucked up than Mickeys.'

'Right.'

'So you want me to keep you company, is that it?'

'Isn't that why you came?' He chuckled, sardonic. 'I want more than that. I want you to keep me sane.'

I was to work on the *cantina*. I was to help turn it into a studio. I would go down with him each day, dismantle the huge old vats so we could get them out the door, clean the place up, cover the walls with paint. I would have my own tools. He would teach me to saw and plane. Giosetta pulled a vicious, dog-like face when he told her that.

'*Và a cagare!*' she spat.

She had marched onto the balcony to discuss my wage.

'Are you crazy? You're going to *teach* her? I want nothing to do with it! Go and shit!'

She stood there with us, close enough now that I could smell her: musk, garlic, anger. I wondered if she could smell me. Dust, sweat, desire.

'Don't worry, *mamma*,' Jula said to her. 'You worry too much. She needs the money. She can help me do the job.'

'Why not put her in the groves?' the old woman cried. 'Why do you need her here at all?'

'I don't want to put her in the groves, *mamma*. When was the last time I asked anything of you?'

She couldn't bear to look at me. I stared at the ground; I made diamond patterns in the dirt with my foot. When she opened her mouth a third time, showing her stained teeth and cursing again, Jula took her by the arm. He led her down on to the fruit paths and away. Lola followed them, hopping – first on one foot and then the other. I watched them walk along the grove-side. I saw Giosetta lean on Jula's shoulder to shake a stone from her shoe, all the time coughing and spitting; shaking her head and saying: '*Julito*, I thought you were happy! *Caro mio*, I just don't understand!'

Her hair was fine and cropped short like a man's. But she was dressed like a girl. She wore a red silk scarf around her neck and a little skirt that showed her old knees. I watched them as they withdrew into the orange crop. Her words rose above the short green trees.

'Are you retarded? Are you blind, my idiot son? How did she find you here? Where did you meet her?'

'Does it matter?'

'You met her in the casino!'

'I don't go to the casino. That's Ana's thing. Stop asking questions, *mamma*. Please.'

'Please, please! Who the hell is she? Do you plan to marry her, is that it, put a ring on her finger? Tell me, *figlio mio*, how do you expect this to end?'

A sudden wind came up from the valley; it rushed around my ears. If Jula spoke at all then, I didn't hear what he said.

That night he showed me the designs. He rolled the papers out flat on the floor of his room; we kneeled before them on the cold, red tiles.

'She wants it all to change,' he said. 'She says too much bad stuff has happened here. And she's getting old; she's rheumatic. She hates the damp and the dark.'

So his plans were full of light: doors unhinged, walls knocked out, new windows in each room. The old, black stone would be painted white; whole floors would be demolished, new echoes made.

'You're a real architect!' I said.

'Just a student for a while.'

I traced the words he had pencilled, meticulous in the plan margins.

BIANCO. BIANCO. ABBATTA. METTA GIÙ.

He showed me the rooms – the finished ones. The new library with its great ladders and shelves big enough to walk along. His mother's attic – on the opposite wing to Jula's –

her golden walls and blue velvet drapes swinging down on to the floors. Then Analisa's room: bare-walled, clothes all over the floor. A full-length mirror built into the north alcove, the glass smeared with fingermarks. A single, unmade bed.

'So you quit Mickeys?' he asked as we walked down the back stairs and out under the arches. 'What happened? Was Mickey being a prick?'

'It wasn't that so much,' I told him. 'I didn't like where I lived.'

'Via Soreca, eh?'

My face burned red.

'You knew where I *was*?'

'Word gets around. My brother has a big mouth. I thought it might be you when he told me. It wasn't that I was asking. Savio said Paolo had some English girl living with him. I don't know many Brits in Catania. Who speak good Italian. Who look like you. You know you won't earn half as much here as you did in the club, don't you? Not even a third. Nor a quarter.'

'I don't care about that,' I told him.

'And I don't care where you've been living. Or who with. Want a beer?' he said. 'Want me to show you the groves?'

The two of us treading the paths; eating cold, young fruit. Crossing ditches, climbing walls; breaking branches underfoot. Him beckoning, me following in the spring evening light.

6

It was dark by the time we got back. Jula said I could sleep downstairs. He took me into a small room – filled, almost, by two huge armchairs. Jula said it was the old servants' quarters. He showed me a bell on the wall. The ceiling was beamed and low. There was a fire burning. In the shadows I saw Lola, curled up asleep in a fruit box. She had her arms wrapped around a skinny greyhound. At her feet was my hat.

'His name's Mondo,' Jula said, bending over and stroking the dog. He took a blanket from the back of one of the chairs and draped it over the box. 'He had a brother called Paradiso. He got shot. Now you're all alone Mondo, *che peccato*!'

I took a blanket too. 'He's yours?'

'He's Lola's.'

Jula disappeared for a while and came back with pillows and sheets. Then he brought wine from the cellar, cold chicken and bread. We ate quick. We hardly talked at all. I lay down by the fire. The next thing I remember, Jula was standing at my feet.

'*Sogni d'oro,*' he was saying.

Dreams of gold. I looked at him standing there above me. He had his shirt off. Faded blue tattoos covered his arms. I wanted to reach up and touch them.

'*Sogni d'oro,*' I whispered back.

I watched him as he left. I heard the wind whirl down the chimney. His footsteps as he went upstairs. Then I slipped into dreams.

It must have been past midnight when Analisa walked in. I awoke to the sounds of her stumbling around. I opened my eyes and leaned up on both my palms. She was standing in the doorway with her hair straggling over her face trying to light a cigarette.

'*Ciao*,' she mumbled.

She bent over the dog-box and gave Lola a kiss. Then she turned to me.

'I can't believe you made it in,' she said, sinking down into one of the chairs and letting her arms swing over the sides. Her voice was husky, her words slurred.

'Made it in?'

'That she gave you your job! What do you want here, anyway? If it's Jula, you'll pay. He's had a hundred women, more! He's been too afraid to bring any of them here.'

'What is there to fear?' I asked – but she didn't answer.

Her eyes rolled back in her head. Sweat shone on her brow; her breathing turned deep. There was no point trying to talk to her.

I had another dream. Jula's hundred women appeared before me. They were pale and naked; they were like ghosts. I walked amongst them. I gave each one a gift. A mandarin, an apple, a lemon, a pear: I placed a fruit in the cup of each pair of white hands. *Thank you*, they mouthed. *Good luck!* All the women did the same – except the last: the hundredth. She didn't thank me. She made a snorting noise.

She was fat and dark; her belly was slack. She shook her body; her breasts swung. Her nipples wept; her sex was a mass of grey hair. I gave her an orange. She ate it whole. She took my chin between her finger and thumb.

'Kiss me,' she said.

So I opened my mouth and I kissed her. I kissed her to make her go away. Instead she took my lip between her teeth and bit me. I pulled back in horror: I had a mouth full of blood. I tried to speak. I couldn't; I had a mouth full of stones. I spat them out and screamed. No sound came. I screamed again and woke up. I was shivering. For a moment I didn't know where I was. I was sweating and shaking with cold.

The fire was almost out. The room was very dark. My eyes stung with smoke. I could hear Lola breathing; I could hear the dog. I looked up at the armchairs. Analisa was still there. In the darkness, she looked strange. I strained my eyes. She was motionless.

I listened for her breath; I heard nothing. I sat up next to her; her cigarette was burned down to the butt. I knocked it from between her fingers; it was just a stick of ash. I moved closer and took Analisa's lighter from her lap. Then I lit it in front of her face. Her lips looked a rosy blue.

I paused. Then I leaned over and slapped her. I thought I heard something and slapped her again. She moved her head from side to side like she was dreaming. Then suddenly, like someone only half-alive, she lunged forward and punched me pathetically in the chest.

'Fuck off,' she gurgled, her eyes opening into soft, grey slits. 'Leave me alone, will you? Get away.'

'I thought you'd stopped breathing,' I said.

'What? Where's my cigarette?'

'Look,' I said. 'I thought you'd gone over. And if you want to know, I'm not one of Jula's girls. I came here for a job. I needed work.'

'I'll believe that,' she smiled, deliriously, 'if you really want me to. But whether I do or not won't help you, Marlena. My mother never will.'

She closed her eyes again and started snoring. I laid back down and looked into the fire. The last flames flickered like little mouths; I watched them dance themselves away. Then I lit a candle on the hearth and pulled the rug up to my neck. I watched Analisa through the night.

7

The *cantina* was out to the north of the farm and behind it, hidden in a glade, a mile or so beyond the woodshed. To get there you left the arches from the back and took a rocky path downhill. It was wild in that direction, steep; the grasses were snake-filled and tall. Adders wound across the stones; brambles and thorns strangled the way. You needed good shoes – for sections of the path dropped jagged; others sloped water-smooth. There were points where – if you didn't squat – you had to thrust both arms out at your sides, like wings; half-balancing, half-falling. Or as Lola used to say, making the Aeroplane Man.

Eventually the path flattened and split. At the place where it forked grew a mulberry tree. Climbing up on to the lowest branch you could sit, unseen, with the trunk at your back – with Etna behind you and ahead of you, the north-east coast. Looking down from the hills the Mediterranean looked so still – and an unreal green. Sometimes it was the colour of grass in the mornings; sometimes the colour of turquoise stone.

If you managed to scale the mulberry trunk and reach the branch above, you could stand and peer over the hedge-tops to see along the right-hand track. That way was level and straight; it was overgrown with nettles. It ended with a metal gate. The *cantina* was down the left-hand path, which dropped sharp again after the fork, winding down the hill. It was right out of view. You couldn't see it standing on the tree-branches or from any high place on the plot. Even close up as you turned the final bend you might accidentally pass it by – for it was set low in the earth, covered in ivy and magnolia. The only clues that something had been built down there were the small white doves which flitted from holes high up in the barn wall. If you didn't see them, or if you saw them and didn't think, you might keep on walking until you reached the stile, and jump down, unaware, on to the road to Motta Camastra.

Wine is altered by light; in the sun it just sours. The small holes in the *cantina* wall weren't windows; they were there to circulate new air.

'Our main problem will be sight,' Jula told me on the night we looked over the plans. 'We'll need oil lamps – a dozen. Maybe a generator too. It'll be hard going, Marlena – you ever worked all day in the dark?'

I pictured back rooms, back alleys and club basements. 'Yes.'

Across the entrance to the *cantina* was a thick brown bolt. Shifting it with both hands and pushing on the doors you stood, at once, at the top of a flight of steps. There were twelve of them. They ran into the darkness and were slippy with damp. They had no rail. From the air-holes in the wall sunbeams crossed the barn like searchlights – but they were too high to be of any use to us. To be able to see at all in the *cantina* bottom, you had to wedge the main doors open with a bottle or a rock. Even then, towards the back of the place, you had to feel your way around. It made me uneasy, walking into pitch black like that. The first time I went down there I felt powerless, blind.

In front of the stairway were the vats – six of them. There were three in a row to the left of the steps and three more to the right. Each one was massive, raised on bricks; each had a wooden ladder at the head. That way, thirty years ago, a man could have climbed up there to do repairs – or set a bottle on the ladder-top and started the tap.

'We need to take them apart completely,' Jula told me. 'We need to take out everything. We'll clear the floor; I can put in a scaffold. Then I'll work on the rafters. I'll go up on to the roof.'

'It's impossible, Jula!' I cried. 'This can't be a studio – it's set so low! How will you see – even with windows? We're barely above the ground.'

No, he said. It was not impossible. Not if the roof was made from glass. He would scythe the magnolia, he told me – and pull off the slate. Then he would put in skylights and let the day come hammering in.

Dismantling the vats took the whole of May. Savio said it should have taken a lot less. Not that he knew anything about it; he hardly ever came down to the barn. He didn't work. He was never out of bed before noon. Then he used to get up and go down to the shed in his nightclothes. He would sit there and smoke, waiting for us to return. I got used to the sight of him in his slippers and gown, cross-legged on the cutting-stump, the wood axe loose in his free hand. I knew the noises he made as he sat there, restless, muttering like a madman and hacking idly at the ground.

'Been down there again?' he would jeer, as we came back from the *cantina*, sweat and wine dust on our arms and faces. 'The two of you, all alone? Fancy that – Marina and Julito! The labourers! *Gli innamorati!*'

We ignored Savio. We didn't rush. The vats were ancient; Jula wanted to preserve them. He would rebuild all of them, he insisted, if the wood was good. He said we should be tender with the past. But things don't ever turn out how you plan them – and the barrels were no different. We saved only two. I still don't know if Jula ever built them up again.

We started at the back of the *cantina*, the darkest end. The first four vats were useless; they were rotten all the way through. When we tried bare-handed to prise the belt-planks away they split into pieces; the kegs rocked like ships on water and then caved in. There was nothing we could have done. We were forced to step back and yell as they came, first rumbling then creaking then crashing down, flooding the floor and spattering our faces with soft splinters and red silt. Each time it happened, we spent the hours that followed piling the sodden wood into crates and carrying them up the stairs. We dried the pieces in the sun. Jula built a fire with them on the rocks. He was burning history, he said. It was the only time I ever heard him talk of regret.

The two vats that survived were empty. With no wine inside them they had stayed pretty dry. That made them easy to take apart: the belts didn't snap; the planks loosened when we jostled the barrel-ends. We carried the saved wood out on our backs. We laid it in two groups on the grass. Some planks were etched with numbers or had words written along them in chalk. Many of them bore a figure and then said 'LEFT' or 'RIGHT'. One plank read only: 'SCHIGGHIAPED'.

Once the vats were gone and we had used a siphon to drain the inches of spilled wine from the floor, we found other things in the *cantina*. A couple of rusty oil lamps, a knife, a pair of boots; a wartime comic gone mouldy under the bricks. Jula picked up a metal hip flask with thumb-marks around the middle; he cleaned it out and filled it up. And in the storeroom at the back of the barn we found fourteen glass bottles, deep green and round and the size of lorry wheels. Some of them still had their corks: some were full; most were stinking and stained burgundy-black. We hauled them out, bending our knees – Jula hugging the base and staggering backwards up the steps whilst I gripped both my hands to the neck. Outside we emptied the bottles, poured the old wine into the weeds. Then with wire brushes we scoured them back to green.

He was right: Jula was capable of doing the whole job himself. It was hard for me; my body clock had been turned on its head. I was used to working the afternoons, the nights. Now we got up at first light. In the beginning I seemed to do nothing but rest, to talk to Jula as he moved wood and bricks and machinery, to smoke, to try and wake myself up. I sat and listened to the tales of his life: their small, ordinary details rippling through me like stones being dropped into a well.

By the time the vats were out, I was another girl. I had learned to love the daylight, the air, the being outside at the start of day. The look of me had changed. My hair had turned white-blond, my shoulders had browned and broadened, my hands had grown cracked and rough. I have a photograph of myself at that time; Jula took it. I am cleaning one of the big green bottles, standing in front of him with my legs apart. I am bending over the bottle and smiling up into his face. I have a rag in my hand, and a wire brush; my hair is stuffed under a cap. It's hard to believe that it is me – I look so boylike, young. In the picture I am unrecognizable. I am grinning at Jula like a lad.

One morning in May I had gone out under the arches to the stove. I was the first one up. I stood spooning coffee into the pot. It was early, blue-dark; a few watery bands of colour had begun claiming the sky. Jula came up behind me, silent; he smelled of sleep. He put his hands on my shoulders; I tightened the lid. I struck a match and set the coffee to boil. Jula squeezed the tops of my arms as the gas flames puffed to blue. He cupped his palms over my muscles; I tensed them in a joke to show my new-found strength. But he didn't smile; he only pressed his fingers on my skin.

'You are no longer a dancer,' he said.

8

I never asked Savio why he wasn't in the army. I didn't
speak to him that much. But I was curious. He wore all
the gear: the khakis, the boots, the military tags. And like
all the army boys he had a shaved head. Up at the farm he
used to roam around like a sergeant, shouting orders to
the local boys who worked in the groves. He would speed
down the lanes on the quad bike, timing himself with a
stop-clock. At night he watched the track.

Every evening he'd stand at the far end of the veranda
with a pair of black binoculars. Some nights he spent
hours there, watching. At first I thought he was looking
for wild birds, spotting the rare white owls which moved
like phantoms through the dusk. I had been at the farm a
while before I figured out what he was really doing. I had
to follow him.

One night during supper I made up some excuse. As
usual Savio had left the table whilst the rest of us were still
eating. Hearing him lift the latch of the balcony door I got
up; I tiptoed down the hall. When I reached the library I
stopped; he'd left the door open. I could see him easily from
there. I climbed a ladder and sat up on one of the huge
bookshelves Jula had made. The smell of wood and leather
hung around me. The air was cold.

Savio stood there for a long time doing nothing. He just
kept clicking his boot heels together. His breath bloomed

ash-white in the night. He began humming – a dim, mechanical tune – then he stopped and jerked forward. Way in front of him, at the point where the dirt track met the lane – a pair of car headlights appeared, blinking their yellowgold before the dark. They lit the yews that lined the road. Like a secret code, they seemed to wink from every bend. I don't know where they were headed. Maybe the Barba farm, or beyond. Jula said there was a house still standing up on the old, cracked road, the one that toured the volcano, marking its last habitable edge. Maybe the car was making its way there, I don't know.

'Thieves!' Savio yelled out. 'Criminals!'

He kicked the ground with his boot.

'I can see you – you bastards! Thieving scum!'

He spat, furious; he lifted the binoculars to his eyes again. The car just wound along the forest wall. At the brow of the hill, it dipped and vanished. I jumped from the shelf. Savio growled under his breath; I went back along the hall, left him shouting obscenities down towards the gate.

When Jula first introduced me to Savio he just stared at me, deadpan. I had been at the farm a couple of days by then, working. The three of us were standing under the arches. Savio acted like we had never met. I had seen him a hundred times at Via Soreca; he knew exactly who I was.

'Why would he do that?' I asked Jula.

'Because he wants you.'

He used to click his fingers to get my attention. If there were people around he would call me another name. Marta, Mona, Marina – as if he couldn't quite remember what mine was. Wherever Jula and I were working, he was always there too: humming, smoking cigarettes. He would come and find fault; then he would go to Giosetta and complain. We used too much money. We took too much time. Wouldn't it be cheaper to bring in a pro? In one whole summer I never saw Savio do a day's work. He just hung on the back of Jula's plans. Trying to control them, to make them his own.

I avoided Savio. When I was alone with him he came too close. He put his hands on my shoulders, or around my waist; once he touched my face. He would bring up Mickeys; call me the stripper girl.

'Dance your dance,' he would say and he would laugh.

Jula said he carried a knife. If I saw him coming before he saw me I walked the opposite way. If I was alone and I heard his voice boom through the house I would stay perfectly quiet and still. I'd push my door shut and bolt it as if the price for being found there was my life. Then I would count the slats of the rattling blind, the summer flies buzzing around my face or – *one, two, three, four* – the number of times he would shout my name. My right name, that is – the name I knew he knew – before he would give up and go stumbling down to the still. *Marlena, Marlena, Marlena, Marlena*: each time louder and more insistent than the last.

9

Most afternoons we did business down in town. We bought some things, sold others; sometimes we worked for Jula's friends. We would come back from the *cantina* and wash, eat; then we would load the tools on to the truck. Jula drove; I sat beside him. We would talk to each other then, raising our voices above the rattle of the engine.

Jula spoke of the Sicily he knew as a boy; of his friendships then, his ideas. He talked about architecture, art; how he had once dreamed of being a painter. Out of everyone, he said, it was Van Gogh he loved the best. He had seen *The Starry Night*. In the silences I would lean out of the windows, see the hot air rising from the roads. In that kind of heat the crops seemed to cry.

The visors in the truck were broken. Jula wore Analisa's shades. They were big and purple, shaped like cartoon hearts. They made Jula look like a girl. He asked me questions. I mapped out my life for him. First kiss, first hit, first trick: Jula never seemed to mind what I said. I loved those short, bright trips through the valley with him. On them I learned I had found a man who did not need me to tell lies.

The pickup didn't belong to Ana – it was Jula's, but he said she needed it most. She was grateful for that, in her strange, junkie way; she left messages – sometimes half-smoked cigarettes – for him to find the next day by the wheel. I used to try and imagine her coming home from Nina's in the early hours of the morning – with Franco's gear in her pocket and a fix only moments away. I used to think of her fumbling around in her pockets for spare smokes for Jula, smearing her shabby thanks to him in lipstick on the back of a casino bar bill.

'ONE OF THESE DAYS, BROTHER!' was her favourite thing to write.

One of these days.

'What about Lola?' I once asked Jula.

'She's all right,' he told me. 'She's tough.'

'If it were me I'd be piss-bored,' I said. 'She's just hanging around.'

'What can I do?'

'I don't know.'

'What do you think she wants?'

'To be with you.'

'That's not true.'

'Jula, you're the only one who gives a fuck.'

'Okay,' he answered. 'Okay.'

So he invited Lola to come and work with us. He went out to the well where she sat most days, chucking gravel down into the water.

'But what will I do?' she asked, picking the grit from her palms.

'You're good with numbers aren't you? You can take care of the book.'

'The book?'

'The account book.'

Lola's mouth curled with joy.

'It's the perfect position for you, Miss Schiggiapeddi! You can be our money-man.'

She leapt from the well-rim then, landing on all fours like a cat.

'Money-man!' she proclaimed, running down the hill and around the side of the farm.

We followed her to the pickup and all got in; she wriggled between us. Jula turned the ignition key. He rolled the van slowly down the track. Lola slapped her hands on to her bare knees.

'So where are we going?' she cried. 'What do I have to do?'

'Well – first we're going to Fiorelli's to look at his old saw. Then we're heading for Jack's. What's important, Lola, is for you to watch the budget. The saw we buy today can cost no more than eighty thousand lire.' He looked at her very serious. 'Can you remember that?'

'Don't be silly, *zio* Jula! Of course I can!'

So Jula reached into his shirt pocket and handed her the cash book. It was small, black, leather-bound. It was thin and worn.

'Give me something to write with!' she yelled. 'Let me get that saw stuff down! *Zio* Jula, I'm the money-man! And this is my money-man book!'

We had reached the lane; Jula put on the brakes. He reached into his pocket again. Then he pushed Lola's thick black hair back with two fingers and slid his drawing pencil behind her ear.

It wasn't long before Lola took part in everything. She started getting up in the mornings and following me out to the stove. She made the coffee for us; she washed the pot. She would have rolled Jula's cigarettes if he had let her. Each day as we descended the *cantina* path she reeled off questions. Had we ordered more plaster; covered the wood? Had we got round to fixing the mixer yet? She wouldn't come inside – she said she was afraid of stepping down into the dark. Instead she waited for us outside in the shade of the trees, making calls and appointments for Jula on his mobile phone.

After lunch we'd travel into town. If we were buying equipment we would arrive at the house – of Dino Fiorelli or Mario Fiera or whoever it was we were trading with that day – and Lola would stride out the back with Jula to inspect the gear for sale. I used to follow them, listening to Jula talk her through the clues to what was a good buy – and what was not. Lola always used to walk slightly behind him, gazing up at him like a disciple – one hand clutching the account book, the other making a determined fist. I used to love to watch them haggling together; bringing down the price of the goods with murmurs and stern shakes of the head. When Jula gave his silent nod Lola would write the final number down with her pencil as he pulled a wad of bank notes from his jeans and counted them one by one.

Mostly we worked in Francavilla; in Motta Camastra and the hills around the farm. Sometimes, though, we drove down to Taormina. Then, I would lean out the truck window and cast my eyes along the streets. I would look for the Zepelli family; I don't know why. I guess I thought I might see Paolo's sisters, or the *zia* shuffling down the promenade. Maybe I would even glimpse old *zio*, soothe his misery with a smile. But it never happened; I never saw any of them.

'They're too good for this part of town,' Jula said.

For we were not in old Taormina any more; we were way beyond the *piazza* – far from the big hotels and cobbled stones. We were low down, in the new town, close to the sea – where the warehouses and saunas were; where you could rent rooms by the hour. Jula's friends were all poor; they shared flats in the red-light patch, or lived in trailers on the site. Most of them were artists trying to sell their work. Some of them dealt dope, too, or other stuff; this French guy Jula knew faked tickets for the trains. It was funny, Jula knew so many strangers. He said it made him feel he knew the world. The truth was he had never even left Sicily.

'You've not even crossed to the mainland?'

'Maybe next year,' he said.

We worked for these two Danes once – a couple of painter guys who lived down by the station. They were queer, for sure. Jula knew them through Lukáš. They didn't speak much Italian, so they couldn't pick up work; they spent their summers trawling the beaches selling watercolours of Taormina – then they starved all winter, sketching and knocking up frames. Anyway, they had moved into this coldwater place, it was an old massage parlour. It was a crazy flat all right; walking in there for the first time made me think of home. There were mirrors on all the ceilings and a bed which shook when you flicked a switch. The walls and floors were painted in gold and black and red.

Arriving with our things – with the stepladder and tools – we climbed two flights of stairs. Jula went ahead of me, taking most of the ladder-weight, smiling, glancing back. At the top of the steps was a glass door. It had a woman painted on it, a girl in silhouette. She was naked, big-breasted; she was pointing towards the buzzer. Jula pressed it. It played that old tune 'Je T'aime Moi Non Plus'. I burst into reels of laughter, I reached and put my hand on his shoulder.

'Jesus Christ,' he said.

The Danes were organized. They were like all Scandinavians, Jula whispered as the door opened and they both appeared, showered, shirt-smart. We followed them through the parlour rooms and they showed us what they wanted done. They made the job easy. They had covered everything with old bedsheets, labelled their belongings with room-names and stacked them along one side of the hall.

'You know we've no money,' they reminded Jula, as he was breaking up the mirrors.

He waved them away. So they ran around us, blond-haired and ruddy-faced, sweeping up shards and bringing us endless cups of coffee and shouting: '*Tak! Tak!*'

I had worked with some Scandinavian girls at Mickeys. I had known Danish men too. And the guys spoke a bit of English; they spoke English like Americans do. In the evening they cooked for us. We ate fish and drank bottles of Danish beer. Then just as we were about to leave – our tools at the door, the flat colour-stripped and bare – one of them, Lars, I think his name was, led us into the hall, beaming.

'*Ta-da!*' he cried.

He pulled a bedsheet dramatically off a pile labelled WORKSHOP. Dust moved around us in a sparkling cloud. Jula coughed; I wiped my eyes. It was the framing gear under there, the wood; the equipment the guys used to make up their pictures.

'Help yourselves,' said Lars. 'Please – take all you need.'

Jula was puzzled.

'We don't need frames,' he said.

'But for your skylights?' Lars asked, pointing eagerly behind the wood to something wrapped in plastic and thick brown tape. 'For the roof of your *cantina*?'

He was still smiling, his mouth half-open, cherry-red, as Jula slashed the tape with his penknife and pushed a finger through the hole. He grinned. It was the way things worked and Jula liked it. The Danes had paid us in sheet glass.

10

Lukáš was queer too; he was another *ricchione*. When he wasn't down at Libost he was out on the *scala* with Nikki Battisti, the guy whose barn Jula torched as a kid. He just laughed about that now; he said it was years ago. We spent a lot of time with him. Nikki never let us down.

Jula said they were all fucked up – as a couple, I mean. He said there was always some drama. Nikki was three times Lukáš' age. It made him nuts. He didn't want Lukáš to go out. He didn't want him to have any friends. I suppose at the bottom of it all he just didn't want to be an old man. I couldn't see it at first. I thought they seemed happy. It wasn't until I had been to the *scala* a few times that I realized that Nikki was always drunk.

One afternoon we got a call from him. He was pissed, wailing down the mobile. He wanted us to come and fix his septic tank. The backyard was flooded. The tank was leaking.

'He says there's shit everywhere,' Jula told me, packing a torch and rubber gloves.

He sat in the back of the pickup and pulled on a pair of green wellington boots. Then he reached under the seat and pulled out another pair – smaller, bright orange, belonging to Analisa.

'Here,' he laughed, throwing them on to the ground. 'Better put these on.'

Nikki's place was almost derelict. It was right on the *scala* edge. He only lived in one half of the house; the other half had no roof. It had bushes growing up over the walls; the stone was all covered in purple moss. And there were cats everywhere – Siamese, Burmese, rescue cats, strays.

'Save my little darlings!' Nikki howled to us from the doorway as we pulled up on the gravel.

He was standing there in his dressing gown with a bottle of Schnapps, a kitten clinging to his shoulder. He looked his age, dressed like that. The skin sagged from his arms in rags.

'*Ciao amici!*' he cried as we got to the door, kissing us both on our cheeks.

He stank of booze and cat piss; he was shaky on his feet.

'Hello Nikki,' I said.

Inside the house, Jula put on the gloves. He had grabbed them from the sink when he got the call. They were too small for his big hands: a woman's size; they were tight and pink. I laughed at him. He went down into the cellar; he asked Nikki to turn the water off. Then he went outside with his torch to get a look under the tank.

'Don't go, Marlena!' Nikki pleaded as I got up to follow him in my orange boots. 'Don't leave me alone!'

'Where's Lukáš?' I asked.

'Just keep me company, please!'

So I took pity on him and sat down. He pulled a bottle of red wine from the rack.

We faced one another at the kitchen table. Nikki drank a garbled toast. The cats surrounded us; halfway through the bottle Nikki went to get his bird. He had this talking mynah bird; he kept it by the door. He put his knobbed hand inside the cage. It hopped on to his finger.

'Sing to me Sonny,' Nikki said. 'Take away my blues.'

'What's up?' I asked. 'Nikki, don't worry about the tank.'

'Oh, it's not the tank,' he groaned, his eyes all watery red.

The cats brushed around his legs, sticking up their tails. The bird began to sing.

It turned out some kid from Catania had been to the *scala* looking for Lukáš. He wouldn't say what he wanted. He wouldn't give Nikki his name.

'Some little Romeo! And so pretty, so young! My days are numbered! I'm just a pathetic old fag!'

'Maybe they're not fucking,' I said, hopefully.

The bird hopped on to the table, chirping: '*Fucking! Fucking!*'

'Do you honestly think that? *Honestly?* Then why the big secret? What else can it be?'

When Jula returned I left the room. I heard him start to talk to Nikki about screws and pipes. There was music coming from upstairs. I went and knocked on the bedroom door.

'Lukáš? Can you hear me?'

It was locked from the inside.

'Lukáš, it's Marlena. I'm here with Jula. It's only me.'

Lukáš slid the bolt across. I waited for him to appear but he didn't. I knocked again and pushed the door open. Then I saw him. He was wired. He was strutting around the room in his underpants with his jaw clenched. Jimi Hendrix blasting out of a blown speaker. Lukáš yowled 'Manic Depression' at me through his blond curls. He was holding a little glass pipe in his hand.

'Hey!' he shouted, as if I might be deaf. 'How's it going, Marlena? Hey, Marlena! Come in and sit down!'

'I'm here with Jula,' I told him. 'We're checking out the tank.' I stepped into the room and sat on the bed.

'What tank?'

He took a first lick on the pipe, inhaling until his chest made him look like a cartoon hero.

'You want some?' he said, once he got a chance to breathe. 'I tell you, Marlena, there's nothing like it!'

'I know, I know. But that stuff fucks me up.'

He started dancing like a freak. His eyes bulged. His arm and legs jerked; robotic.

'Fucks me up too! Yeah man!'

I wanted to talk to him more but there was no point. I had found Lukáš' new love. The room was a tip: there were bottles, scales, lighters, foils; little piles of rock wrapped in plastic on the floor.

'You doing business?' I asked.

'Maybe I am. So what? Maybe I'm not. What's it to you?'

'Don't be like that,' I said. 'You'd better watch out, that's all. Nikki might be old but he isn't stupid. You've got people coming here. He knows something is up.'

'Yeah, yeah,' Lukas answered.

I looked at him and caught his glance. 'Yeah.'

Then the music changed and it was 'Hey Joe'. Lukáš started to dance slowly behind me. He made the shape of a wheel with his soft, pale hands and let it turn invisible around my skull.

'Doesn't matter what I do,' he said. 'You see, there's no rules, Marlena. Life is a crown, it goes turning around. A golden crown turning around and around.'

'It's nice to see you,' I said.

'You don't mean that.'

'Yeah I do.'

'You do?'

'Christ, Lukáš. That stone's going to your head.'

He started singing, all pseudo-mad: '*Gonna shoot my baby!*'

I stood up to leave. As I closed the door behind me, I heard him laughing. Then he turned the music off and the bolt slid back.

Downstairs Jula had cleared up the mess. He was explaining it to Nikki, who was trying hard to focus. The piping under the tank had rusted at the join.

'I've taped it up for now and put a pan under. But it won't hold for long – you need new copper pipes. They're not cheap; I'll try the metal yard. Just don't flush the toilets, okay? And keep emptying the pan. I'll come back the day after tomorrow.'

As he saw us to the door Nikki began to giggle.

'What? Don't flush the bogs? *Ever again?*'

'Jesus, Nikki – can you just not do it?'

He came out and stood in his bare feet on the gravel.

'You're good kids,' he rambled. 'But do me a favour – don't start anything! Life's a bitch – it's horrible, terrible! But love will kill you! Love stinks!'

I I

The metal yard was run by a bunch of Czech and Slovak gypsies who lived behind the northern beaches. It was the new site Jula had talked about. Most people called it the Black Wreck. Surrounded on all sides by eucalyptus, the wreck ran along an inlet bank; it was a narrow strip of wasteland the colour of Etna rock. Driving along the road to Messina or walking on the sands below you couldn't see the site; it was concealed, like a treasure or a black secret. The only way you could tell it was there was by looking upwards, to the sky, where trails of woodsmoke rose in the mornings through the bittersweet-smelling trees.

Apart from the scrapheap – which filled the far end of the yard – there were maybe fifteen trailers on the site. Most of them were battered and small. Only one of them was new. Each of them had its plot marked out with funny tin windmills or sticks with rags tied around them, driven into the ground. Each van had junk piling up around it and a chimney with a hat. Cats slept on the trailer roofs; a dog lay in the shade. There was a horse, too, a white pony – tied up with a long blue rope near the stream. He had real horseshoes on his feet. His name was Lux.

Sometimes you would see Lux being driven through the towns, through Calatabiano, Taormina, with the scrap-cart at his back. Some of the Italian kids threw stones as the cart passed, yelling: *Stranieri! Loschi! Feccia!* But not all of them were so dumb. Some just stood still, watching from the roadside, wishing they had metal to give as the driver called for copper, iron, tin.

Going down there that day for Nikki's pipes, we found the wreck deserted. The sun was high; heat seemed to push down on to the strip.

'They'll be sleeping,' Jula said, swinging the pickup around and parking it next to an old green Audi. I glanced into the car, saw a couple of kids dozing in the back. When they heard the truck they scrambled out.

'*To je Jula!*' one of them cried, whacking the bonnet and shouting: '*Boom boom boom!*'

The other boy sloped up to the truck.

'*Čau, Julo,*' he said softly. '*Dejmesu cigaretku.*'

He peered in through the open window. Jula offered him his pack of Marlboros. He took one – and then another for his brother. The boys disappeared into the Audi and slammed the door. I watched them striking matches on the dashboard, heard them laughing, coughing – until eventually the car filled up with a screen of brownish smoke.

When we got out Jula pointed to the new trailer. It was made from chrome. It glinted in the sun. It was longer than the others – by maybe twenty feet. It had a flat metal roof and red geraniums round it in pots. We walked towards it; together we crossed the yard. Jula tapped on the trailer door with the truck key.

'*Alex, vole! Jste tam?*'

A groan came from inside; the top half of the door opened. An older man with heavy brown eyes and a deep scar on his forehead leaned out on his elbows.

'Jula!' he chuckled. 'I haven't seen you in six months! I was dreaming in there, all alone! I was dreaming I had a woman! Maybe somewhere in the world she was dreaming she had me! What time is it? Tell me, what can we do for you? How is your mother these days? Is she still knocking the old place down?'

'Can I look through the scrap?' Jula asked, stepping up. 'I need some piping for Nikki Battisti's tank.'

'What kind of piping? Copper? You want to catch up first? You and the new lady want some tea?'

He bent down and pulled on the bottom door.

'My name is Marlena,' I said.

I followed Jula up the trailer steps and as I did a memory shot through me. The van was filled with ornaments, crystal. It reminded me at once of Dana. I wanted to let out a stream of questions. Do you know Dana Pourová? Does she come here? Have you seen her? I scanned the gilt-framed portaits lining the trailer walls and recognized no one. I sat down at a table. Jula sat on the bed.

The man Alex filled a kettle. He was stocky, dressed in a suit and cravat.

'I've known this one since he was born!' he said, looking at Jula and slapping him on the back. He seized Jula's fingers and gripped them tight. 'And his father, too – what a fiddler! What a man! Julius, he was the spit of you!'

Jula nodded, indifferent.

'The spit of you, I say!'

We drank our tea. The air cooled. Eventually we heard voices, laughter; the slamming of trailer doors.

'I think I've got the pipes you need,' Alex told us, draining his cup.

'I'll stay here,' I said, as he and Jula walked into the sun.

I don't know what made me say that. Jula threw me his smokes and I sat down on the van step. I watched the men as they strolled over to the scrap-pile and started poking around under the skeleton of an old car. Then I lost sight of them as they squatted behind it. A soft warmth rippled down the wreck now; the boys who had been in the Audi sauntered over with some younger kids. They wanted more cigarettes. I gave them some. Then the women came.

There were four then five then six. They were hard-faced. They encircled me. They came close; they all had these black tattoos. They started clicking their tongues on the roofs of their mouths and saying something I'd heard somewhere before.

'*Bílá, žena bílá!*'

I stood up.

'*Bílá!*'

'What do you want?' I asked

One of the women reached over and touched my hair. Another came closer; she pulled at my skirt.

'Leave me alone,' I said to her.

She made the clicking sound and pulled again. With them crowding round me like that I felt I couldn't breathe. I was hot. I decided to go and wait at the truck. I pushed past the women; they let me go. They didn't need to follow me. They had won. They watched me from the other side of the yard. I couldn't see Jula anywhere. I took out a cigarette. A few gypsy girls came and loitered at my back. I handed them a smoke to share and we watched a pair of black butterflies twisting in the sun. They spiralled round our heads. The girls cooed as they danced in the smoke and flittered on to the ground.

Then it happened. A young boy shot out from behind us. He shoved past and stamped on one of the creatures. It lay there motionless in the dust. He was quick, and mean; he did it again. He turned, he whooped; I knew that sound. He bent down over the butterfly and pulled off a wing; he started jumping up and down with it, his fingers all powdery black. I knew him. It was Kuba.

'Hey! Kuba!' I shouted, but he ran off behind the vans.

I walked back, breathing quick, into the middle of the yard. I watched him darting through the eucalyptus trees and across the stream-bed. I ran after him now, but suddenly the women were there again, making a wall with their bodies. They wouldn't let me pass.

'I know him; I know Dana!' I cried – but it was too late. Kuba had disappeared.

The women bundled around me. Then they took me by the arm and walked. They ushered me to the pickup truck.

12

The next morning I awoke in my bed downstairs to find the sun already high. The room was bright; Lola was gone from the dog-box. Under the sheets and sheepskins my body had started to sweat. I couldn't understand it; Jula hadn't mentioned anything. I cast my mind back to the drive home from the wreck. We had talked things over then. The plan had been this: we would work in the *cantina* until noon – we'd cover the floor with new concrete. Then after lunch we would take the pipes out to Nikki and Jula would fix the tank.

I sat up and stared into the fireplace. My head hurt with too much sleep. I pulled on my work-clothes; I walked out on to the arches. White-blue light glinted in from east and west. It was near midday. I tied my hair back; I drank cold water from the tap. Then I set off down to the *cantina*, noticing as I stepped down from the rear arch that Ana's shutters were closed. She was back from Nina's; she was in. But the pickup truck wasn't there.

Walking along the barn path I kept looking over my shoulder. I kept thinking I heard footsteps. Man-laughter filled my head. But each time I stopped, there was nothing, no one – just the throb of crickets in the scrub. At the fork I climbed the old mulberry; I saw only more bushes and trees. Why hadn't they woken me? Where was the truck? Squatting up there on the second branch my thoughts began to quicken. Dropping on all fours on to the left-hand path, I broke into a run.

Turning the bend on to the clearing I slowed right down. I strained my eyes then stopped. The *cantina* doors were wedged open. The generator was soundless; Jula's workbench was covered over. An empty loading trolley stood in the sun. Fumbling for my box of matches I walked towards the barn across the grass.

'Jula?' I said when I reached the stair-top. 'What are you doing without any light?'

'Sweet thing!' came a voice. 'What are *you* doing all alone?'

My chest thump-thumped. The voice did not belong to Jula.

'My brother's out of town, *carina*! The shit has finally hit the fan!'

'Where is he?' I demanded.

Savio didn't answer. I stepped down into the dark.

'Where?'

'My, my!' Savio mocked. 'Why the concern?'

I was at the step-bottom now; still I couldn't see him. I put my arms out in front of my body.

'Just tell me!' I said.

Suddenly he stepped from nowhere into the shaft of doorway light.

'If you must know, the cement-mixer is done for! You'll never finish your project now – you'll have to knock the damned thing down!'

'So where is he?' I repeated. 'Where's Lola?'

'Oh, all right. I suppose I'll have to tell you. They've gone to Messina to try and get another.'

I walked up to the mouth of the mixer; I smelled yesterday's cement. A few of Jula's tools lay around the machine: a saw, a palette, a plane. I ran my fingers along the mixer-rim; the tips turned instantly to white. Then I started: a female voice cut the darkness. I swung around and faced Giosetta. She had been standing in the shadows all along.

'That thing needs moving, girl; get the trolley down here.'

'Why didn't he take me?' I said.

She came and stood next to her firstborn son.

'Because with a new machine in it, *straniera*, the truck wouldn't take your weight! Come on now; earn your wages! You'll work for Savio today if you want to stay.'

She started walking up the steps in her high-heels. I waited for her to slip. I watched her old hips shift; I saw her eyes glimmer down when she reached the top.

'The trolley,' she said.

She clicked her fingers. I put both my hands on to the mixer and gaped into the broken drum.

By the time we had lifted the machine up the stairs, Giosetta was gone. My belly wheeled. I was alone with him. We dragged the mixer from the trolley on to the grass. Savio sat on the ground and wiped his forehead; I turned and headed back to the barn. But he stopped me. He had other plans. He whistled me back.

'What is it?' I asked.

'We are not working here today. I've something else for you to do. Something to suit you. You are going to clean!'

He got up. He came over and pushed the bolt across the *cantina* doors. Then he laughed and started striding back up the path.

'I'm not a maid,' I said.

But I wanted Jula then more than I have ever wanted anything. With no more protest I followed him back to the farm.

*

I had never been into Savio's room before. To get to it you climbed a flight of metal steps. They ran up the outside of the building on the east side of the house; they ended at a door made from plywood and net.

'Take off your shoes,' he said at the threshold. 'Make sure your feet are clean.'

My bare soles burned on hot iron as I brushed the dirt from them and stepped in.

Inside, the room was small and spotless. The bed was perfectly made. Show cabinets lined the walls; little keys hung shining from the locks. Behind the polished glass doors stood rows of silver cups – and Savio's binoculars, sleek and black.

'Why have you brought me here?' I asked. 'There's nothing that needs cleaning.'

'Really, women are so hasty! Marlena, why don't you calm down? Why don't you like me? Why can't we be friends? Let us begin again. I think we have simply got off to a bad start.'

He patted the bed three times with his right hand.

'Well? What do you think of that?'

'I have no interest in your friendship,' I said.

I stayed standing. His smile vanished. I walked barefoot to the door. But Savio blocked my way.

'Okay,' I mumbled. 'What is it I have to do?'

He reached down under the bed. I looked at his stooping body; his brute, brown arms. He stood up sharp, holding a roll of army canvas in one hand. He let it swing down to show a set of knives. He said: 'Now, darling, can you see? I want you to clean my babies.'

He gave me a bottle of yellow oil and a dusting rag. I should go from base to tip, he told me. The blades should shine. He was just about to demonstrate when in the distance we heard Giosetta. She was shouting his name: *'Savio! Savio!'*

'What, mother? Can't it wait?'

He turned to me, his face twitching with irritation.

'I'll be back.'

He left the room and shut the door – then he jammed a plank of wood across it from outside. I didn't try to stop him. I didn't shout. I sat, locked in Savio's room, with my hands in my lap on the bed. I listened to the sound of his footsteps. As he walked coolly around to the front of the farm, answering his mother's call.

There were nine knives; they were all different in size. With Savio gone I pulled out the biggest one. The metal curved slightly, scythe-like; the handle was made from bone. I caught sight of my face-shape in the blade: my tanning skin, my pale blue eyes. Then I stood up with the knife in both hands, cutting the air like a swordsman. Messina wasn't that far. I wasn't going to clean. Jula would be back soon.

Walking over to the cabinets I opened one. I peered in at the cups: they all bore Savio's name. They were for fishing, hunting, archery. One was for some kind of race in a car. Other knives were in there too. Then a hand grenade, the binoculars; a black hip flask. I wanted to touch them, I wanted to touch everything. Instead I closed the cabinet door. With the rag I wiped my prints from the glass and sat back down.

An hour passed. Two. Savio didn't return. I grew bored with waiting, restless. I kneeled up on the bed. I smoothed the sheets with my palms; they were tucked in neat. Then I leaned over the bed and took a peek underneath. There were boxes there, all filled with clothes. I looked through some of them; they were ironed and clean. Then I slipped my hand under the mattress, found a book on guns, a magazine full of women with their legs apart.

I went over to the window. I tried to scan the lanes for the truck – but it was too far, the light was bright; I couldn't really see. It was then that I thought of the binoculars. With my finger and thumb I turned one of the cabinet keys.

They were heavy. They were in a leather box. I took them out and unwound the strap. I hung them around my neck. Lifting them up to my eyes everything blurred; I twisted the dials with my one free hand. And I smiled to myself, for I had escaped now: I was standing at the roadside where the high stile crossed the forest wall. In a magnified dream I was waiting for Jula; in the cool pine shadow I stood on the bends. I didn't hear Savio come back up the steps or take the plank from the door. I didn't hear him come in.

'Looking for love?' he said.

Out of fright I let go of the binoculars. They swung and hit my breasts. The strap chafed my neck. I steadied myself, raising my chin.

'No,' I answered. 'Just looking.'

Now he jammed the plank on the inside of the door.

'Snooping is so undignified,' he said.

He walked over to me and lifted the binoculars from my neck. I felt my heartbeat in my fingertips. I swallowed hard. Savio opened the glass cabinet; he put the binoculars back in. Then he took out the hip flask; he shook it. He unscrewed the silver cap.

'Drink,' he said.

He was very close to me now. He took off his glasses. His eyes looked very wide. I took a swig from the bottle, tasted whisky.

'Again.'

And he kept on saying it: '*Bèvilo! Bèvilo!*' – until my chest was drink-hot and my cheeks were numb. He made me stand there and drink like that until the flask was empty. Then he slid his glasses back on, replaced the cap and slumped on to the bed.

I watched him as he turned on the TV with his remote control. He started flicking through the channels; he turned the volume up.

'You know, if my mother finds out about you two she'll fire you,' he scoffed. 'Wouldn't that be a shame?'

I was drink-dizzy, slurring my words.

'I don't know what you mean.'

'You'd better watch out, Marlena. He's *mamma*'s precious boy!'

'And you?' I asked Savio. 'What exactly are you worth?'

His face tightened. I sniggered and turned away. I was too drunk to be afraid of him. I didn't care what he might do. I touched the plank; he jumped from the bed very quick. He pulled the TV plug from the mains and grabbed me by the arm.

'*If you fuck him, I'll kill him,*' he growled through his teeth. '*I'll kill both of you. Understand?*'

He snatched the knife-set from the windowsill. He shook it, I watched it unroll. He came close to me. From the top pouch he pulled out the smallest blade. He let it flick in and out – three times, four times, all but touching my skin. Then he tucked it into his boot sock and pulled the plank from the door.

'Thank you for your work, Marina. Oh, by the way – Paolo's coming tonight. I've invited him to play *scopa*. He and I against you and the mongrel. Who do you think will win, *carina*? Better straighten up!'

I walked outside into the midday sun. I was weak-legged. I stumbled down the stairs. I turned the corner to the front of the farm. I felt a yell in my throat when I glimpsed the pickup coming speeding up the lanes. I jumped over the herb gardens; I ran down along the track. I reached the gate and climbed over it and there he was, Jula, leaning out of the truck window, one arm on the wheel, sweat on his forehead and the heart-glasses sliding down his nose.

'*Ciao,*' he said. 'Enjoy the morning? I thought you could do with the extra sleep. Anyway, the mixer's had it and the trip was useless; I couldn't get what I wanted. I'll have to go back. I've got the pipes in the boot; I'm going to take them to Nikki's.'

'Are you going there now?' I panted.

'I could do, I guess. He'll have to feed us; we're starving.'

'Starving!' echoed Lola. 'We haven't eaten a bean!'

'Are you all right, Marlena?' Jula asked. 'You look wasted!'

'Take me with you,' I said.

13

My body is accustomed to the games men play. It re-covers quick. It can match any pace. I slept in the truck, my back to Lola and Jula, my head bumping on the rattling glass. When I woke up I was near-sober. The engine had stopped. Opening my eyes I could see the sea out my window. A pair of clammy child-hands were tickling my neck.

'Marlena, *zia* Marlena! We're at *Signor* Battisti's. We're here! *Zia* Marlena! It's time for you to get up!'

I turned around. Lola was kneeling next to me. The driver door was open. Jula was sliding the copper piping on to the ground.

'Didn't know you were a morning drinker,' he said.

'I only had one. It must have been the heat.'

'*Zia* Marlena's a morning drinker!' Lola chimed.

'Enough,' scolded Jula. 'And enough with the *zia*. Lola, you've got to stop calling her that. It isn't funny. It isn't her name.'

'*Zia* Marlena and *zio* Jula! My uncle and my aunt!'

We carried the pipes on our shoulders. My head was throbbing; my mouth was dry. On the walk up the drive all I could think of was water – but I was out of luck. The front door was shut. Jula frowned. He rang the bell. There was no answer.

'They knew we were coming,' he said.

Then I heard a noise. Jula heard it too. It was dull and far off. Someone was shouting.

'For Christ's sake,' said Jula, shaking his head. 'They're having another fight.'

'Could we come back tomorrow?'

'We can't. The join will have burst by then.'

'Why are they arguing?' asked Lola. 'Will there be another flood?'

We laid the pipes upon the ground and walked around the back. The shouting was much louder now, hysterical. It was Nikki. He was crying, shouting over and over: 'Talk to me, you stupid fuck!'

He was in Lukáš's room. The window was open.

'Hey Nikki!' Jula called.

'*Talk to me!*'

We walked through weeds and wildflowers to the abandoned part of the house. Jula pushed on a door covered in creepers; a couple of cats shot out of the musty dark. We ducked our heads and climbed a staircase. The floorboards were full of holes. Bats hung from the ceiling, sleeping in rows; Lola gasped when she saw them. We went through a second door and we were back in the light.

'Nikki!' Jula called again. 'What's up?'

Nikki kept on sobbing. We walked towards the room.

'Come out of there,' Jula said. 'We've got the stuff. What are you doing? What's going on?'

Around the corner we heard Nikki shuffle on to the landing and moan. Then he appeared before us, swaying in his green silk gown. He was even more pissed than the last time we were there. His gown was gaping open.

'What's the *matter* with him?' Lola whispered. 'I can see his *pipi*!'

Nikki's cock dangled in front of us like a withered rose.

'Cover yourself up!' Jula shouted, but Nikki paid no attention.

'Come and see my fallen angel! Come and see what he's finally done!'

Walking into the room I smelled the unmistakeable smell of cooked heroin. It was sour, metallic; it filled me with longing. I wanted to cry out then. Lukáš was on his back on the bed. He had a needle hanging in the crook of his left arm. His arm was swollen; his fingers were dark purple. His leather belt was still tied tight around his muscle.

'Take that off him,' I said.

Nikki jumped; he started wailing and wringing his hands. I went over to Lukáš and unhooked the belt myself.

'Is he all right?' Nikki cried. 'Should I call for help? Is he dying? Is he dead?'

'Sit down,' said Jula. 'Lola, go and wait in the hall.'

'Is this man like my *papà*?' Lola asked.

'Just wait outside for us!'

'My darling! My baby boy! Why would he do this? *Why?*'

I bent over Lukáš; he was all right. He was warm. Sweat-drops clustered along his hairline like beads of glass. A pale rose colour tinged his cheeks; I listened to his breath.

'Should I call for help?'

'No.'

I took the needle from Lukáš' vein and placed it on the shelf.

'Why not?' Nikki went on. 'How do you know he's okay?'

'Because I do, Nikki. He'll be fine now that thing is off.'

'I'm going to call them anyway.'

'I wouldn't – not unless you want him banged up.'

'What are you talking about?'

'Look around you! Nikki, you need to get a grip on things. That boy who came here that day, the cute one. He wasn't coming for Lukáš. He was coming to score Lukáš' stuff.'

I gestured around the room. To the money, the scales, the bags of heroin; the cans, the yellow lumps of rock.

'What are you saying? Is he in that deep?'

'Deep enough to be dealing,' I said.

I stayed with Nikki. I led him back down the stairs. Jula took Lola out to help him fix the tank. I kept checking on Lukáš, for Nikki's sake – but he was okay. After a couple of hours we heard him creaking around upstairs.

'Leave him a while,' I told Nikki – but he marched up there and started to rant. I followed him.

'How did you get in here?' Lukáš spat.

'Your secret's out! You forgot to lock your door!'

Nikki picked up a handful of bags and waved them in Lukáš' face.

'What the fuck is this?' he screamed.

'Get out of my face, man.'

'How dare you! You're living in my house!'

Lukáš laughed then.

'I can hardly do it at the club,' he said. 'Look, no one will find out. We're miles from anywhere. Come on, Nikki; I'm making a mint.' Then he gestured to the wine glass in Nikki's hand, adding: 'Don't tell me you couldn't use the cash.'

When Lukáš said that, Nikki lost it. He tore open one of the wraps and started spraying gear all over the floor. Then he did the same with another. Lukáš ran and punched him. Nikki fell on his side, blood welling around his lip.

'Get out!' he cried. 'Get out of my house! Go now – or I swear I'll call the police!'

'Yeah right. The police. You don't have the guts.'

Nikki took his mobile from the pocket of his gown and dialled the number.

'Turn it off,' I told him – but he wouldn't.

We heard a woman's voice on the other end. Lukáš ran at Nikki again; he grabbed the phone and hurled it out of the window.

'You're a little shit!' Nikki screamed.

'And you're a hypocrite! Look, man, I can stop. Don't kick me out. We go back years, yeah? I'll stop selling the stuff, all right? Don't kick me out. What will I do? Nikki, listen to me. Where will I go?'

'I don't care! I don't believe what you say! It all makes sense to me now. The way you disappear!'

'What, and that's worse than being a wino? I'm not a junkie you know. Tell him, Marlena. Tell him it isn't like that.'

I looked at Lukáš then, at him pleading with me with his heavy-lidded eyes.

'Next time,' I said, 'just take off the strap.'

14

'*Scopare*' means 'to sweep' in Italian, 'to take the prize'. It also means 'to fuck'. *Scopa* is an old Sicilian card game; it's played in two pairs. The aim itself is simple: you take a partner and your task, between you, is to win points by taking the suit of cups. The catch is that together you must beat your rivals without ever seeing what your comrade holds. Most Sicilians know how to play – although some will tell you it's a game of chance. They are plain wrong; I played on the *scala* for a whole summer. To take a round of *scopa* you only need to know your partner well.

By the time we got back from Nikki's it was evening. The sun was glowing in the west. Savio was setting up the card table under the cedar tree, covering it with a piece of green baize. I watched him from the pickup as he smoothed down the felt; fastidious. He picked off the specks of dust and dirt; then in the centre of the table he placed a metal pot. Neither Jula nor I spoke to him. Jula was too stirred up about the thing with Lukáš. He said he was going down to the *cantina*. He was going to try and fix the cement-mixer himself.

'I'll be back in time for the start,' he said, sadly.

'How will you know? Will I come down?'

'There's no need. I'll keep an ear out.'

'For what?'

'For Paolo's bike.'

So I left him to go alone. I went and sat on the veranda with Lola. In the end we got our own game started; she wanted me to play pairs. We knelt down on the floor; she spread her set of square red cards face down over the concrete slabs. She explained the rules; she said I had to turn over two cards at a time. If they didn't match up, she said, I should put them back. It was easy enough – but my focus kept slipping. She won pair after pair while I got stuck trying to retrace a circus clown.

Then just as I thought I had found it I heard the Ducati. I glimpsed Paolo's bright orange helmet; I saw the bike turn on to the track. I stood up, reluctant; I leaned against the rail.

'Do you know him?' Lola asked.

'I guess.'

Paolo drove to the side of the farm. He got off the motorbike and climbed up the balcony steps as Lola took her turn. He pulled off his helmet; his curls bounced around his face. With an eagerness I couldn't fathom he came and kissed me on the cheek. I stepped back; he smelled of starch and fresh sweat.

'*Ciao, ex-moglie!*' he said.

He giggled to himself at the joke. He was all dressed up in a shirt and tie.

'Why the get-up?' I asked dryly.

'What's the matter, Marlena? Aren't you pleased I'm here?'

'I can't tell yet. I don't think so,' I said.

His mouth fell open.

'Clown!' cried Lola, holding up the matching card.

Paolo kept on calling me his ex-wife; he wouldn't let it go.

'You've got to quit that horseshit,' I told him as we walked down the barn path.

He had begged me to talk to him alone before the game. It made no difference to me. I wanted to see Jula in any case.

'Okay,' I said. 'I'll show you the *cantina*.'

So he stumbled after me down the track. He was wearing his brogues; he kept sliding and slipping.

'What's going on here anyway?' he called to me. 'Why did you come?'

I swung around and smiled.

'I came to do a job,' I said. 'I'm getting paid, you know.'

'What do you mean, you're getting paid?'

'I'm working here, with Jula.'

Paolo looked flustered.

'Well, he doesn't need a partner! Attempting construction work, Marlena – really, it's ridiculous! And you don't need to go back to Mickeys either. I've passed my final year.'

'So what?'

'So what? So I've got my degree! No more cheap affairs, no more dancing – and no more working for Jula! I want you to come and live with me again. I want you to come to Milan.'

We had reached the fork in the path. I leaned stunned against the old mulberry tree. I looked at Paolo; I had to fight the urge to slap him. I decided not to take him to the *cantina* after all. Instead I took the orchard track.

It was flat that way; we got down there quick. Once we passed through the green iron gate the ground rose up in tiers. The grasses around us were long and dry; the whole place was overgrown. Cherry trees grew in lines of six or seven. Mashed red fruit lay rotting beneath them.

'It stinks down here,' Paolo complained, lifting his trousers above his shoes.

Flies buzzed around his ankles; I walked on ahead. He followed me along the orchard steps to where I stood on the highest tier. He started fumbling around in his pockets.

'Well?' he stammered when he got to the top.

'Well what?'

'Are you going to accept?'

'Paolo, what on earth are you talking about?'

'I've come to take you back!'

'I'm not coming back,' I cried. 'I don't *want* to go to Milan. Who have you been talking to – Savio? What has he been saying?'

Paolo pulled his fist out from his pocket and unclasped it. On his palm lay a small gold ring.

'That you miss me! That you'll marry me!'

'You're a fool,' I replied. 'That's just not true.'

But he wouldn't leave it alone.

'Try the ring on,' he said.

He took my hand and pulled at it.

'*Try* it!'

I yanked my hand back. He locked his arms around my waist then and started to kiss my neck. I smelled the sweat and the starch again.

'Come on, *ex-moglie*! Marry me!'

I drew in breath. I couldn't take any more. I brought my right knee up to my waist. He was tugging at my clothes. I slammed my heel down on to his shin. He let go; I turned and kicked him in the balls. He squealed like a girl; he fell to the ground.

'I've lost it!' he cried. 'I've lost the ring!'

I watched him writhing around in the grass. I assumed it was over. I started walking along the top tier wall towards the gate. But when I looked over my shoulder he was up again – and he was running after me; he had found the ring. He was holding it triumphantly in his hand – he looked like a maniac; he was smiling with glee. His fingers were smeared with red pulp. He caught up with me and with them he grabbed the collar of my shirt. I staggered back; I turned around quick. I tried to punch Paolo in the face. But I was off-balance: he ducked – and it was then that I fell. I tumbled down over the drystone wall and landed on the tier below.

'You piece of shit!' I winced. I had fallen on to my wrist. Pain shot up my arm. I stood up swift.

'Marlena, I'm sorry. I didn't mean it!'

My legs and arms were covered in fruit.

'Get away from me you fucking idiot!'

I started wiping myself down with a handful of dead grass.

'Marlena –'

'You make me want to be throw up.'

His face crumpled.

'You had a flat I could stay in, that was all. That's the only reason we ever spoke. Now leave me alone, will you? Go back to Catania.'

Paolo hung his head. He put the ring back in his pocket and started to cry. He had dirt all over his cheek; his shirt and tie were stained dark red. I walked with him snivelling behind. I spoke to him only once after that; it was as we passed the woodshed. I realized there was something I needed from him.

'Tell me Paolo, have you seen Dana?'

He straightened his tie and tucked in his shirt, thinking he was back in with a chance.

'She's been evicted,' he said, smugly. 'I saw her the day she left the block. She was loading her things into a horse's cart. She was making her kids sit in the back. Did you ever give her money? If you did then you're a fool. You see, Marlena – I was right about her! She hadn't paid a single day's rent!'

15

Savio called for the best of three games of *scopa*. As the sun sank red behind the forest line, Jula and I claimed the first. It was easy for us; our opposition was weak. We didn't use any of our best tricks. We didn't even need fortune on our side. Savio was on the ball – he was as sharp-eyed as ever – but Paolo was useless. He couldn't keep up. He was drinking too much for a start; he kept downing shots, then taking the vodka bottle and filling his glass right up to the rim. He spent the game mooning at me over the table instead of watching the round drop down; then he would bring the ring out from his pocket and flash it, trying to make me sorry, trying in vain to catch my eye. In the end I turned and grimaced at him. He forced a feeble smile. Then he fanned his cards in front of his chest in an attempt to hide the cherry stains on his shirt.

'What's the matter with you?' Savio growled at him. 'Are you still not over your broken heart?'

'You conned me into this!' Paolo bleated.

'I haven't the faintest idea what you mean!'

'You know what I'm talking about. You must have planned the whole thing!'

'All I know is we're losing – to a spell of lover's luck!'

Paolo hiccupped and poured another drink.

'Pull yourself together!' Savio snapped.

I picked up the ace and let the knave of swords fall. And Jula was looking at me – and he was almost laughing. It was too late for them. The game, I knew, was won.

Jula spread his set of gold steadily over the baize. He held them all but two: I revealed the ace and the jack. Savio shouted out; Lola poked her head out from her place under the table and banged with her fists on the covered wood.

'Hurray for *zio* Jula!' she cried. '*Forza zia Marlena!*'

'*Zia* Marlena?' Paolo whimpered. '*Aunt?* What does she mean?'

Not even Savio bothered to answer him.

'*Scopa,*' I said.

Savio changed the plan after that. He switched seats and refused to play alongside Paolo; he couldn't stomach another loss. He got edgy about the old Sicilian cards; he sent Lola up to his room to fetch a regular pack. The ones she brought down were new, still wrapped in their cover. They smelled of plastic. They had birds of prey painted on the back.

'Game two – out of three!' Savio declared, pulling out the pack jokers and tossing them aside.

'We'll play poker,' he said. 'And we'll double the stakes. Ace high, fours wild. Every man for himself.'

With a cigarette held fast between his teeth he dealt out the new cards and snatched up his own hand. He slapped a hundred thousand lire note upon the felt. To my relief Jula winked at me; he reached into his back pocket and threw the same into the pot.

'Anyone else going to match me?' Savio cried.

Paolo put in his share. I looked at my cards. I looked at Jula. Then I shook my head and pushed back my chair.

I'm not afraid to live – but I'm not much of a gambler. I knew I couldn't go on. My hand was poor; in my head the rules of poker were a haze. Savio let out a shriek of mockery as I placed my cards under my empty glass. I didn't care. I stood up and walked away. And that was when I got my picture: I took the Nikon from where it hung on the back of Jula's chair and fastened it around my neck. I went and stood at a distance from them – up on the south arch step. Shadows fell behind me; the last of the day's light bled magenta on to the stone. I prised the lens cap off with my fingers; I checked the meter. Then with a jerk of my thumb I wound the camera film on.

I didn't need to watch the game; I knew the outcome all right. I could tell how it would end just from the way that Jula sat. He was leaning back in his chair, half-smiling; his shoulders were loose, his set of cards already face down on the table. I held the Nikon up to my eye; I brought him into focus. The night was over. The money was ours.

Some things are fated; I'm sure of that. When they come to you, you recognize them as yours; it's as if they have been happening to you all along. We bought pizza that night with the first note from our winnings. We left Savio and Paolo to sit and bicker; we got in the van and counted the prize. Analisa was only working midnight to four by then; it was her one shift. She was sick of doing tricks, Jula said. She was cutting down on gear, trying to quit. We promised her to be back by eleven; we drove down into Calatabiano to some takeaway called *The Golden Cheese*. When we got to the place it was packed out. I stayed in the truck.

I smoked and turned the radio on. It was Coltrane playing. Tapping out jazz-rhythms on my knees I watched Jula through the plate-glass window; I saw him looking up at the menu board like an ordinary man. And I remember how a married couple strolled past the pickup. A young man and woman wearing golden rings, dressed in their smartest clothes. Who knows where they were going; their black heels clicked together. They seemed to walk along in perfect time – as if they had learned to dance. They had their arms around each other tight; I watched them stop to kiss and touch. Then they set off again, strict tempo; they teased each other as they passed me by. Jula came out of the takeaway and opened the truck door. He leaned over and placed a hot pizza box on my lap.

'I got you the *Valentina*,' he said as he climbed into his seat.

I opened my box and looked into it; the van windows steamed up with heat.

'It's with extra chilli – is that OK?'

I bit into a slice, green peppers tingling on my tongue.

We ate in silence. We wiped the grease from our mouths with the backs of our hands. When we had finished we threw the boxes on the pickup floor; then we drove to the all-night supermarket and bought a couple of cold beers. As we headed up through Calatabiano I glanced at the truck clock. We had two hours until eleven – until Ana had to go. I swigged from an open bottle; we passed under the bridge. And it was then – under its long, black shadow – hot-mouthed, with my heart jumping – that I said: 'Let's not go home yet. Jula, let's not go back.'

He nodded in assent. He swung the pickup left on to an uphill track. I had never been that way before; the road was narrow, straight. We drove along it for a few miles passing no one. When the track forked we went left again. I smelled pine in the air: we had reached the south edge of the forest. Trees rose above us now in shifting walls of black.

Jula dropped gears; we were all the time climbing. The truck rattled over a grid. He wound open the canvas roof;

I looked up through the gap: I saw a new moon and stars. I put my head back to the sky and stretched my hand out to the bank. Long, damp grasses met my fingers. The pine-tops shushed in the wind.

We barely spoke as we crossed the forest. We reached the peak of the hill. The track levelled; a patch of dull orange light bloomed on the brow. It looked electric; I couldn't understand it. I leaned forward onto the dash-board and put my hands to the windscreen.

'What is it?' I whispered, 'a city? I thought we were miles from anywhere!'

'We are,' said Jula as we moved into the glow.

'Is it an airport? A stadium?'

Then I stopped asking questions, for we had left the forest behind us. We had reached a plateau. Four great flood-lights came into view. Then: high wire fences in the pattern of diamonds, a gate with a busted lock. A smashed-up kiosk with a red-and-white striped barrier; a picture of a man wearing a hard hat; a buckled warning sign.

Jula stopped the truck at the kiosk and switched the engine off.

'It's the old marble quarry,' he said.

We got out and ducked under the barrier. We began walking along a curved, white road. I looked down to the ground; sometimes I had to turn my back – for the wind came in sheets, blowing the hair from our faces, leaving thick white dust on our mouths and eyes. It covered our clothes; it whipped itself up and stung my skin. We kept going; we came close to the quarry-side. The cables slapped the light-tops as we reached a vast white hole cut deep into the earth.

I pulled my coat collar up around my neck and walked towards the edge of the pit. I gazed down into the rock-body, saw dozens of criss-cross lines where the marble had been split. There was a digger down there; its door was open. A little whirlwind span in its jaws. Here, I thought, anything could happen. I looked back.

Jula was still there, standing where I had left him. He shouted something to me and laughed – but his words dropped flat into the space between us and died in the wind. I watched him; he looked child-happy then. In the hollow light his smile was just a black movement on his face. He walked towards me, grinning, slow; he reached me and stood white-lipped at my side. We blinked the dust from our eyes. The cables squealed. Scree whispered around our feet. He said my name; he reached into the neck of my coat. His fingers skimmed the ridge of my collarbone. I closed my eyes; the taste of blasted stone filled my mouth. It was there, at the pit-edge, that he kissed me.

16

Analisa was dressing when I knocked on her door. I had gone to tell her that the van was back. She slid the catch and poked her head into the hall. She was in her underwear; her hair was damp.

'*Minchia*,' she said when she saw me standing there. 'What the hell happened to you?'

I looked down at myself. I was still covered in white marble dust.

'I thought you were going into town!'

'We were. We did. We went to the quarry after.'

'That's some night out.'

'I had a good time, if you want to know.'

'Then you're as crazy as my brother. He really is a freak. Are you doing anything just now? Do you want to come in?'

She was in a good mood. She reached out with a bare arm and dusted down my shoulders. I stepped over the threshold. The air in her room was thick; it smelled of skunk and soap.

'I'm running late,' she told me, sitting on the bed and lighting up a spliff.

I stood with my hands in my pockets and I watched her. She put on a lace-up vest, pulling hard at the strings until her breasts swelled over the top. Then she switched on her hairdryer and hung her head upside down. I sat on the floor and leaned my back against the wall.

'Why the quarry?' she shouted over the dryer.

I tilted my head to match hers and mouthed: 'I don't know.'

When Analisa sat up and turned the machine off she shook her hair down and said: 'Well, who cares where he takes you – even if it is the middle of nowhere. If he loves you, you're lucky. With Jula you can't go wrong.'

Once her hair was dry Analisa brushed it fast. She tied it back with a black plastic rose. She pushed in a pair of stud earrings; she pulled stockings over her knees. Then she took a little mirror from the bedside drawer and studied her thin brown face.

'How many tricks will you do tonight?' I asked, as she took a lipstick from the drawer.

She looked at me, unsteadied.

'I don't know.'

She twisted off the lipstick-top and dragged it slowly along her bottom lip.

'Maybe five or six. What's it to you?'

'Jula says you're trying to quit.'

She pressed her lips together.

'Yeah, I am.'

'You done it before?'

'Why are you asking?'

'Oh, I don't know.'

Ana put the mirror back in the drawer and pushed it shut; she faced me with her hands flat upon her knees. Her lips were bright red now; they were pursed and full. I smiled at her. She took a pair of black stilettos from underneath the bed; she slipped them on and stood up tall.

'Don't tell me you're a junkie!' she cried, wiggling her hips.

'I'm clean,' I told her.

'Since when?'

'Since before I left England.'

'You were working, like me?'

'Till I started dancing.'

'You had to learn to do that?'

'I paid a hundred pounds for a shitty course.'

'Maybe that's something I could do! Before that – you were on the streets?'

'Yeah.'

'That's too bad.'

'Do you only work at Nina's?' I asked her.

'Not always.'

I gazed at her.

'When it gets slow in the week I walk the industrial strip.'

Suddenly we knew each other. Ana beckoned me to her. She lifted the hair at the back of her neck to show a ring of dark blue bruises at the nape.

'What happened?'

'Some guy in a Porsche.'

'Shit.'

'Maybe I'll go cold turkey,' she said.

'Yeah?'

'After I've paid off my debts.'

'To Franco?'

'And the rest.'

She stubbed out her joint in the ashtray.

'Or maybe I won't. Maybe it's written. There's a few guys I owe to now. And I can't work without it.'

'But Jula could help you pay things off,' I said.

'It's not his problem,' she answered. 'So don't go talking to him about it, OK?'

She picked up her cigarettes and bag; together we left the room.

'What do you mean – that it's written?' I asked her at the foot of the stairs.

With her stoned, grey eyes shining she turned to me and began to laugh. It was the most alive I ever saw her.

'Once a junkie always a junkie,' she said.

I walked her down to the truck. I stood there as she drove away, watched the headlights fill the lanes. Returning to the farm Paolo and Savio were still under the tree, drinking; I could hear them arguing out the back. So I went around the front; I looked up at Jula's window. His shutters were drawn. His light was off.

I climbed on to the veranda. I smoked a cigarette. Analisa's voice and the sound of the quarry winds filled my head. When I went to my bed there was a note on my pillow. It was in Jula's writing. It read: 'EARLY START TOMORROW? I WANT TO SHOW YOU SOMETHING.'

17

We rose at four; we dressed in the dark. We worked quietly and swiftly; we had finished in the *cantina* by ten. We locked up the barn, leaving the fresh-laid cement to turn hard and white; we took off our overalls and left them hanging at the door. Then we clambered up the barn path, on to the scrub banks and walked in a cruel heat towards Etna.

Crossing the groves, we hid from the sun. We left the narrow, black fruit paths and stoop-walked under rows of thick-leaved trees; the light fell on us there only in thin, broken rays. We stepped over buckets, cutters and pumps; hosepipes gurgled as they soaked the earth. Sprinklers jittered and span. Every so often Jula would stop at a ditch and lift a pipe-end high above his face until cold water cascaded into his mouth. Then he would bring it up over my mouth too until I too had drunk enough.

At the border of the Schiggiapeddi land we came to a shadeless track. A painted board nailed to a wall on the opposite side told us YOU WILL PASS HEAR WITH REGGRET! SIGNED, BEPPE BARBA. I counted the double letters. I wasn't afraid. I was with Jula. We approached the wall.

Jula made a loop-step with his hands and bunked me over. Balancing on my belly and looking down on to the other side I saw the tops of more trees; I swung with my arms and let myself drop. As I landed I hit a pump tap and let out a cry. Jula dropped next to me with a thud. When I yelped at the pain in my back he put a finger to my lips and shook his head.

'Don't make a sound,' he whispered. 'Barba's a real Mussolini. He's the one who killed Paradiso. He's got a gun.'

With that he took my hand and led me along the edges of the grove. We stopped talking and kept to the wall. It was hard: the trees seemed lower, smaller; the air was heavy now and not as sweet. We were going uphill, too, higher on to the mountain; my clothes and hair became caught in branches if I didn't keep my body down. Whenever this happened Jula would reach back and deftly lift them clear; then we would stand and listen – and move on. When we got hungry he took bread from his pockets. We sat, hunched beneath the mandarin trees; we picked fruit from the crop. We ate in silence; afterwards we didn't sleep or smoke. Before we walked again, we stood alert – but there was nothing to worry about. There was no one around.

Eventually there was a dip in the land and the grove ended. We had reached another track. Beyond it was a small barn; even from a distance I could tell it was another *cantina*. Like the one at the farm, it was set low in the ground. It had two massive doors – and brick-holes to let in the light. As we approached it I looked around me. Flowers and grasses brushed my feet. I smelled honeysuckle, violets. I glanced back over my shoulder. I saw how far we had come. Ahead, Etna didn't seem much bigger – but the farm looked so small. We had walked for miles.

He went ahead of me now. He pushed with his weight on the *cantina* doors. They had no lock; they opened with a groan and we stepped into the dark. The roof was high: yellow shafts of sunlight lit up the tops of huge wine vats. I smelled alcohol, wood – and something else, something heavy and strong. We weren't alone in the barn. There was an animal smell in the air.

Jula closed the doors and the scent grew. He led me across a straw-covered floor – over bottles and coiled hoses – almost to the far wall. There, he looked up, way up, into the rafters. In the blackness, my eyes played tricks on me. For a moment it seemed to me the place was roofless: I thought I saw the night sky, planets, stars. I gazed at Jula – he was focusing on something, staring up into the corner like he knew exactly what was there. He made a low, whistling sound with his lips then started to rub his hands together like he was warming them over a fire. All the time he looked upwards. I set my eyes on the dark. Something plunged from the beams; I heard a sound like a drum, saw a flash of magnificent white.

'*Un gufo!*' I exclaimed, as pale feathers fell all around me, for Jula had summoned an owl.

She seemed to hover there above us for a lifetime. Jula called her by name but I didn't catch it; in my ears all I heard was the beating of wings. The bird was so close to us I could see her hooked beak, the grave way she looked at me. I counted the wingbeats until she rose again; I stood as she circled us over and over – five times, six times, seven times – before gliding back into the dark. Her feathers ruffled in the rafters; dust sparkled in the light. Then silence; nothing. I looked up at Jula and took his face in my hands.

It was then that we heard the noise. We moved away from each other, sharp. My lips turned dry – there was no mistaking the sound. Footsteps. Getting louder. Coming towards us; coming down to the door.

'Shit,' whispered Jula. 'It's him.'

We heard the grim voice of a man. Then a child. There was a dog, too; I could hear it panting. Jula grabbed at my arm and we slipped between the vats.

'I'm going to break your nose, you little cunt!' the man shouted. 'Come out, whoever you are!'

The door swung open and the man roared. Turning my neck I could see them in silhouette: a small boy and his father; a young Alsatian dog. My body went stiff. Jula was right; Beppe Barba owned a shotgun. He was clicking open the barrel and reaching into his pockets. He was slotting cartridges into the chamber.

'Leave it, *papà*,' said the boy. 'It's probably just the birds.'

'Come out, I said! I'm gonna kill you!'

He began to walk around, poking with his gun. He kept tripping up. He couldn't see. The dark was making him angry; he started grunting like a pig.

'It stinks in here,' he shouted, tapping the vats with the gun barrel. 'It reeks!'

He came closer. So close I could hear him wheeze. I thought he might pass us – but he stopped just feet away. He rammed the shotgun under the vat where we were standing, forcing it further and further under the casks – then started rattling it around madly until the barrel hit my ankle bone and began slowly to skim my leg.

I sucked in breath through my teeth; Jula clamped his hand over my mouth. My legs started to shake; he bore his weight down on mine to make me still. I could feel his ribs now, his skin touching my skin; the soft rhythms of his breath and the way his chest muscles tightened when the man bawled: 'Get on your knees, Giuseppe! There's something under there! What are you playing at, boy? For Christ's sake have a look!'

The boy kneeled. This was it, I thought. Beppe Barba was going to find us in his *cantina*; he was going to tie us up and shoot. My mind started to speed – then I heard a noise – and the dog started going crazy and I knew what was coming because Jula's chest softened and he was grinning at me. We had an ally. We had the owl.

She lunged from the rafters. She screeched as if she was defending her brood. She flew into the Alsatian's face and pushed out her talons; the dog was jumping and snapping – then she soared and dive-bombed again.

'See!' shouted the boy. 'I told you!'

'Get away from it!' Barba screamed. 'I'm going to shoot it! I'll kill it!'

He aimed the gun upwards one-handed and started swinging it at the bird.

'Don't, *papà*! Please! Please don't shoot! *Papà!*'

The boy tugged wildly at his father's coat; Barba was forced to turn his head – and the owl vanished in the dark.

'Stinking beast!' Barba screamed into the shadows.

He slapped the child with the back of his hand.

'I didn't want it to die, *papà*! Please, *papà*! I didn't want to see it die!'

Barba ignored him – but he lowered his gun. He glanced around.

'Fucking bird,' he mumbled as he walked back out into the midday sun.

Jula took his hand from my jaw then. I couldn't wait any longer; I pushed my fingers into his mouth. As the voices grew distant I started to laugh. He uncoupled his belt; we fell against the barrel-front. I lifted my skirt; he put his fingers inside me – then with his body he began to push. I felt the barrel-tap at the small of my back; I let out a shiver as it loosened and wine spilled on to the floor. With a little jolt Jula pulled me down and shoved me under the flow. He was in me now; my head was to the ground. Wine and red silt came running on to his back, down his neck and over my face. It trickled to my mouth; it tasted like vinegar. It made me smart. I pulled Jula inward and I pushed him out; he gripped with his arms and sank his face into my hair – and like this we went on in the wine and the hay, until I didn't know who was who. When Jula began to shudder I placed my hands tight in his hands; I looked up and the *cantina* was roofless again. And this time, I swear, I saw the universe above me; I saw the planets, like gods, witnessing us. Jula said my name – 'You OK Marlena?' – then he laughed from his belly and the owl whoo-whooed in the dark. And me, I whoo-whooed back, for the love of life.

18

Desire is a hard thing to have to hide. It hollers for attention. It is a blood-cry in the dark. And after the hour in Barba's barn it owned me; it swept me up and along – flourishing on my skin until everyone turned to look.

Giosetta noticed in an instant. She lingered on the arch-steps in the evenings now: there for a brandy or a book – rambling back upstairs in her slippers and gown only once I had gone to my room – and Jula had gone to his, and the lamps were off. Savio was worse. His room was next to Jula's. Jula said he had stopped watching his TV and that at night he swore he heard him stepping up to the dividing wall.

'With a fucking glass, *te lo giuro*! Just to see if you are there!'

Then one day we were going over the skylight plans. We were up in the top room, sitting with the papers rolled out on the bed. Jula faced me darkly.

'Here, take a look at this,' he said.

He stood up and walked over to a postcard stuck low down on the partition. It was funny; I hadn't seen it there before. It was yellow, orange; I looked closer. It was *Sunflowers* by Van Gogh. Jula took it down to reveal a hole – small, newly-carved and eye-shaped – about four feet up.

'That wasn't here yesterday,' he told me.

And he put the postcard back.

We gave Savio nothing to watch. Mostly we stayed away from the farm. Every day once we were done in the *cantina* we sent Lola back up the path – we watched her turn the corner then doubled down on to the Motta Camastra road. We walked north for fifty yards or so and climbed the opposite stile. We bent our heads, tunnelled our way through thick bushes to a small clearing surrounded by gorse. There were others who went there, for sure. Empty beer cans lay in a pile under the hedge with used rubbers and junkie pins. Graffiti covered the flat rock-slabs which rose a little way up from the grass. I used to lie on them and spread my legs as Jula undid his jeans and pushed up my skirt. I used to feel the warm rock press at my back as he tugged at my hair. I would laugh under him there, shout to the sky.

We never undressed. We were too near the road. From the slabs you could see the make-names of the cars through the brush as they braked on the corner on their way up the hill. Once I thought I saw the frame of a man, standing tall at the grass verge, watching. I cried out; Jula came. I sat up and pulled my skirt down to my knees. But when we scrambled on to the roadside there was no one. Only the blush-blooms and black-eyed-Susans standing trembling in the breeze.

Then one day we went to the beaches. Mondo was sick; Lola was staying at the farm to look after him, she said. I don't know what was wrong with him. He kept throwing up blood. Giosetta had called the vet in Messina. They had advised her to bring him in.

'What will I do, *caro mio*?' she gloomed at Jula. 'He is a heavy beast – and so smelly! I can't manage him all alone.'

'Then wake up Savio, *mamma*, he's doing nothing. Here, get a taxi. I have things I need to see to. I'm sorry. I can't help.'

He gave her all the money he had. He left her standing under the arches, lamenting. The bother of it all. The vet's bill. Jula kissed Lola. He headed for the van. I followed him – and without a word passing between us he drove me down to the northern bays.

As you leave Taormina for Messina, the highway rises sharp. You drive almost at the cliff-edge; you look down on to sea and black rock. For over thirty kilometres the road clings to the coast like that; it sweeps past restaurants, kiosks, deserted bars. Then it dips and swerves sudden at Tremestieri, abandoning the sea.

We parked the truck in a lay-by. There was a picnic table at one end of it – and a line of young pine trees. We ran through them and down a bank; we met a path strewn with green needles and sand. We took it, running still; we stopped to unlace our shoes when we reached the *fiumara*. We crossed it; we climbed big rocks; we came to more, flat and sea-shaped. We walked barefoot on the stone-top. The tide was low; we saw pink jellyfish and small, clear pools – and then we came to a set of wooden steps at the rock-side and there, at the bottom of them, was a tiny bay.

Under the cliff-shadow the sand was cool. The pebbles were small and smooth there. The water was glassy blue. We took off all our clothes and lay in the shade. I loved Jula's soft, olive belly; his tufts of thick, jet hair. We walked to the water. We dipped in our toes, then we waded; we stood waist-deep in the sea. He lifted me in his arms; I hooked my legs around him. Gulls circled in the brilliant light.

It was when Jula let me go for a joke, when I sunk for a second under the waves and surfaced coughing and cursing him – it was then that I had the idea. I shot out of the water and ran to our pile of clothes. I pulled Jula's striped cotton shirt over my head, I zipped and belted his old blue jeans – and with his shoes in one hand I darted back up the steps and over the rocks; I scaled back down the black jags and reached the stream. I waited there, ankle-deep; I was dare-dancing, breathless. I gasped as he appeared on the brow. He was wearing my rose dress. He had my knickers clenched in his fist. He shook his wet hair like a dog. And he started to run.

I fled in hysterical laughter. The dress was stretched to near-splitting. He looked like an old theatre queen. I ran along the needle-path and up through the pines. He ran too. At the roadside he caught me by the hips. He pushed me down on to the truck bonnet; he shoved me against the hot white metal until I agreed to give him back his clothes, until I cried the word: '*Pietà!*'

He smiled then, very soft. He kissed me – then all at once he stopped. He stepped back from me and away from the truck. Still laid on the bonnet in Jula's clothes I turned my head. There it was, coming from the Messina direction, taking the corner slowly in a sheet of heat: a long white taxi with a dog in the passenger seat. A greyhound, poking its head out sadly. Mondo.

We had no time to act. We could only stand and stare. We looked down at ourselves; we began to giggle like infants as the taxi pulled up by the truck.

'Hello *mamma*,' Jula said.

Giosetta eyed us deathly cold. Savio leaned over her shoulder.

'Wipe the smiles from your faces,' he said. 'You're as good as dead.'

Mondo began to whine. Giosetta poked the taxi driver between the shoulder blades with her finger. He revved the engine.

'To the meat-market!' she croaked. 'Enough of this pantomime!'

The driver checked his wing-mirror.

'Come on man, go!'

Suddenly something struck me and I stepped towards the car.

'Wait,' I said, knocking on the roof. 'Where's Lola?'

'I left the child with Analisa,' she said. 'She would have slowed us all down. I am not a nurse!'

'*Mamma!*' Jula cried.

'Six years ago she had a daughter. She must face up to that.'

'What if she can't?' I said.

Giosetta faced me steel-eyed.

'When a slut opens her legs, there will always be a cost.'

19

As we turned under the bridge I heard her. Piercing, desolate, above the noise of the truck: Lola screaming at the pitch of love. Jula heard it too; his cheeks drained of colour. He slammed his foot on the gas. We took one corner, then another; we saw her standing doll-like in the middle of the lanes. Her arms hung limp by her sides.

'What's she doing?' Jula cried as we reached her.

She didn't move, even with the van coming. Her eyes were squeezed shut from the screaming. Her mouth was a red open hole. Jula jumped out of the pickup and stared into Lola's face. He gripped her by the shoulders and shook her. She was at least three kilometres from the farm. She couldn't speak; he picked her up and bundled her into the van. The sound coming from her was unbearable. I pulled her to me.

'What is it, Lola?' I kept asking as we climbed the final hill, her face still pouring with snot and tears.

It was only as we turned on to the track that the words flew out ragged, barely-formed: '*It's – my – mamma.*'

When we reached the farm, Lola refused to come inside. We left her sitting inconsolable on the gravel-stones; we clambered up the east stairs. A hot breeze blew through the house; at the stair-top we heard Ana's door. It was flung open, and moving with the wind, banging on and on against the wall, swinging forward and then back. We approached the threshold. We stood there bewildered, looking in. For there she was, Analisa, crouching at the bedside like a praying child. Her face was buried in the sheets; her trousers were round her knees. The soles of her feet were bloodless blue. Calmly, and as if she were still alive, Jula walked straight to her and knelt at her side.

'Sister,' he said.

In the Etnean foothills word gets around quick. That evening I sat alone up on the scrub banks; I watched the police arrive, the doctor, the coroner. I watched the white taxi returning from town. By the time I climbed down from the verge in the darkness, the farm was full of strangers. I moved among them. There were women of Giosetta's age, dressed in black. Some had walked all the way from Gaggi when they heard the news. They brought baskets full of wild flowers with them. They left small wooden crosses at the door. Nikki was there, drunk. An old boyfriend of Ana's showed up from somewhere near Taormina. He was German; he was a chef in one of the beach hotels; he told me he knew Analisa from before her heroin days.

'Look at the fucking Jesus!' Savio murmured from the veranda when he saw him walking up the track. He was dressed all in white linen, his blond hair down his back. His name was Thomas.

Franco came over too on his bike. He didn't stick around long. He parked at the bottom of the track and sat on the stile. Jula spotted him from the veranda and went down.

'Listen,' he told him. 'I don't think you should come here again.'

'But if there's anything,' Franco whispered, sheepish. 'Anything at all I can do.'

'I'll bear it in mind.'

Franco pushed a bundle of cash into Jula's hands, looking at him with his beady black eyes.

'It was what she gave me yesterday. Sorry, man,' he said.

That night I slept in the top room. I curled up with Jula and Lola under the mosquito net. Lola was sleeping deeply; the doctor had given her a shot. Jula was staring at the ceiling and cursing the summer flies. I lay there next to him. I heard Savio leave his room and start the truck. On the other side of the house I heard Giosetta howling. Hours later, I heard Savio coming back.

The van came up to the side of the farm. The headlights lit the room for a second – then the engine stopped; I listened in the dark. Jula had fallen into a doze; he was mumbling in his dreams. Savio was fumbling around on the outside steps now, taking the plank from his door. I heard two kinds of footsteps walking into the room; some were heavy, some stiletto. I sat up against the wall. He was with a girl. They closed the door behind them. I heard a young, empty voice. I recognized it. I heard furniture moving, music. Then Savio began to grunt.

Without making a sound I got out of bed. I pulled the *Sunflowers* from the wall. I squatted there; I placed my palms on the plaster. I moved closer; I put my eye to the carved hole. There, in orange lamplight, I saw Savio's torso moving between a pair of black legs; I saw breasts with golden hoops, bright yellow hair. I turned around; Jula was stirring.

'What's going on?' he sleep-groaned. 'Who's he with?'

I thought I knew. I took another look just to make sure.

'Kiki, the other hooker from Nina's,' I said.

20

Giosetta didn't want a wake before Analisa's funeral. If you ask me, she was ashamed of the way Ana died. She didn't want the house crowded out with strangers for days and so she asked for the body to be taken away. Instead, Giosetta said she would celebrate Ana's life with a feast. Like a fucked-up Last Supper I guess. I couldn't see how grief and food could mix. But the night before Ana's burial Giosetta wanted to eat a meal of fish.

She kept saying it was going to be perfect: her immaculate goodbye. But she was in no state to do it. She'd been getting hammered on booze in the mornings then going to Ana's room and necking her sleepers. She spent the afternoons wandering around the farm unable to speak. She was way too far gone to cook.

The chef guy Thomas told her not to worry. He said he'd take care of it. I don't know exactly where he came from – but he said he knew the best fish markets around. He stuck to his word: five days after we found Analisa dead he turned up at the farm in his linens again. He stayed the night; he slept downstairs. The next morning he went to Santa Maria for the fish. Jula and I went with him. It was still dark when we set off. We drove down in the van – and I remember feeling bad because it smelled so strongly of Ana in there: of her stale cigarettes and dirty hair and cheap perfume. Thomas didn't notice; I mean, it was years since he had seen her. He just gaped out of the window at the daylight coming, the passing world. But at the wheel Jula looked like he might choke if he tried to inhale. Like he was trying not to breathe.

When we arrived at the quayside the sun was rising. The air was cool and salty there. We stopped at the pier-base. Thomas climbed out and pointed to a strip of beach running below the harbour wall. We edged down a flight of slimy green and black steps. Rows of coloured wooden boats sat lined up on the sand. A crowd of women moved between them, bartering with the fishermen – from the *Carolina* to the *Regina Del Mare*, from the *Bella* to *Il Cielo Blu*. We wandered through the crowd, following Thomas until he stopped at *La Dolorosa*; we watched him peering down gracefully into the hull. He knew the fisherman. They kissed and shook hands. Pointing with a slim finger, Thomas asked: 'The swordfish – how much?'

'That's the best fish of the morning. You want it? For you Thomas, a hundred thousand. You won't find better.'

Thomas turned to us; he almost smiled. He handed over the cash. Jula and I stepped forward to take a closer look at the fish. It was a beautiful animal, its skin a deep, silky blue. Laid out newly-caught on the boat-bottom, it looked like it was still alive.

'Thank you,' I said to Thomas.

'*Danke*,' said Jula.

He had found us the catch with the most radiant skin, the most delicate odour, the clearest eyes.

That afternoon Thomas cut the loin from the swordfish and divided it into steaks. He wrapped each one in foil. Jula built a fire out the back. He placed stones around the coals to stop the flames spreading down the bank. Then he set the fish to grill on a metal grid. Thomas covered the card table in a piece of black cloth. He arranged it with broad knives and thin white candles. Jula brought out chairs.

As the smell of the steaks drifted around the farm, Giosetta appeared. She was dressed all in black: black dress, black hat, black veil. She looked even older then, the girl in her utterly gone. She stepped down from the arches and lifted the veil from her face. Her mouth was bright with lipstick; she had thick-painted eyes and nails. She took one look at the table and threw her arms around Thomas.

'*Ma grazie!*' she wailed.

Savio walked behind her, black-suited, black sunglasses down. Lola came to the table hand-in-hand with Jula, her face pink and patchy with crying for so long. I went inside. I changed from my summer clothes. I put on my only black dress; short and woollen and meant for winter. Then I joined them.

With everyone sitting down, Thomas carried the fish over on a platter. He brought potatoes, stuffed tomatoes; he brought bread, water, wine. He lit the candles and then he himself sat down. He pulled a piece of crumpled paper from his shirt.

'In memory of Analisa Salome Schigghiapeddi,' he said in a breaking voice.

'*Figlia mia!*' cried Giosetta.

'*Sorella mia,*' followed Jula.

Lola whimpered; Savio put his boot up on the table. Then he grabbed a steak from the platter and pulled at the flesh with his teeth.

Thomas couldn't even begin his speech; he kept faltering. In the end he let his notes fall to the table; he put his head in his hands.

'Forgive me,' he whispered – and he started to cry.

Savio banged his fist on the table.

'Enough! I want the faggot to leave!'

Thomas sobbed aloud at that. Jula put an arm around him.

'You pair of twisted fucks!' Savio jeered.

Jula looked up at him in disbelief.

'Look who's talking!' he half-laughed. 'Who are you calling twisted? You're a sick bastard, Savio. Last night we heard you fucking Kiki.'

'*Kiki?*' breathed Giosetta, with a mouthful of fish.

'The other hooker at the casino, *mamma*. The one who worked the shift with Ana.'

Giosetta cried out, white fish-flakes spraying on to her plate. Lola asked: 'What's a hooker?'

Jula locked his eyes on Savio.

'*What's a hooker? What's a hooker?*'

'What your mother was,' spat Savio – and he stood up.

He walked over to Jula very slow. Panic tightened my chest. Savio smiled, pulling a fish bone from between his teeth – then he kicked Jula's chair from under him. Jula fell to the ground on his back. I stood up, my body numb. Sounds flew from my mouth. Thomas had stopped his crying. Lola started beating herself round the face.

'*Zio* Jula!' she shouted, as Jula got himself on to all fours. 'Stop it, *zio* Savio! Leave my *zio* Jula alone!'

Jula crawled to the table side and pulled himself up. But when he was halfway to standing, Savio kicked him in the face. I cried out again; I ran to them. Jula tipped back, bleeding and doubled up on the ground.

'No!' screamed Giosetta, as Savio kicked him again in the balls.

'Look at you, gypsy – you can't even fight back!'

In a rush of pride, Jula lunged at him then. He dragged Savio into the dust by his knees. He started pulling at his hair; he knocked his sunglasses off. He was screaming: 'You're an animal! Analisa hated you!'

Savio snarled; suddenly Jula yelled out and put a hand up to his ear. Savio had bitten him. He pushed Jula on to the grass.

'My dove! My dear!' sang Giosetta as Jula dragged himself away.

I watched him go. It was all I could do. I stood at my chair in my winter dress with my hands fast upon the wood. I watched Thomas leave – I never saw him again. I watched Giosetta running down the lemon bank. And I watched Savio as he sat back at the table and, with brother-blood smeared around his mouth, finished his meal.

2 1

He had gone to the top room; I knew that. I could feel him up there before I ever got to him: brooding, wounded, hurt. The farm was still now: Giosetta and Lola had gone to bed. After finishing what was left of the wine on the table, Savio took off in the truck. I went to Jula; I walked through the rooms full of wood and building junk. I opened the door to the foot of the new stairs and climbed them slowly, tracing with my fingertips the grooves that he had carved careful upon the rail. As I walked along the corridor I heard him mumble dimly.

'Great Britain, is that you?'

He laughed at the joke as I pushed open the door. At first I couldn't see him; he was sitting on the floor in the corner of the room. He was holding a bottle of gin; his eyes were closed. He had his head tilted back against the wall. Around him on the tiles were his tools and his plans. I went and sat beside him.

Jula turned to me and opened his eyes. He took a long swig of gin. His left eye was closing up; it was turning purple. His bottom lip was swollen twice its size. A line of blood ran down from his ear to his collarbone, wetting the black of his jacket and shirt.

'What a swine, eh?' he said when he saw me looking. 'I told you he was all fucked up.'

He knocked the bottleneck carelessly against his teeth.

He did it again. I took the gin away. I put my fingers to Jula's ear. He flinched; then he settled. Jula had bitten down to the cartilage. The lobe was torn and streaming.

Like water from a summer fountain, love gushed from me now. Jula's door was still open – but I didn't care; all my fear was broken and gone. I pushed my dress down over my shoulders and climbed barebacked on to his lap. I ran my hands through his matting hair; I sucked at the open wound. I tasted blood and dirt and bodysalt.

'Marlena.'

On my fingers and lips Jula's blood dried brown. The sun disappeared; the shadows grew weak. The terracotta floor tiles cooled and dimmed. Jula traced the length of my arching spine, drumming out light beats on my skin. I don't know how long we'd been sat there like that when we heard the truck on the lanes. It got closer. We didn't move. It came up to the farm and the engine stopped. I buried my face in the crook of his neck. I hunched into him; he didn't say it and nor did I. The words sat in our mouths like stones. It was only a matter of time, we knew, before I would have to pack my things and go.

22

The next morning I awoke in the attic bed to men's voices on the lanes. I got up, looked out the window. The body was coming back. Thunderstorms had broken the night; there had been inches of rain. I heard the frenzied engine of the hearse. It couldn't manage the track.

Jula pulled on his shirt and quick-walked through the groves; at the junction he stood in the watery light watching the wheels spin. He shouted something to the men from the parlour; they came and placed their hands on the long, black bonnet of the car – then with a jolt and a heave and with one man at the wheel they began pushing the hearse back down the hill. They parked it at the stile. They opened the back. On their shoulders they brought up the box, their funeral clothes spattered in mud. As they passed the veranda, I reached again for my winter dress.

At Giosetta's request the coffin was laid under the arches. With long, gold-coloured ropes they lowered it down on to the stone. They were red-faced from the feat; they dabbed handkerchiefs at their heads. Lola stood and stared at them as they sweated and wheezed. Giosetta nudged her.

'Manners, Lola!'

And she handed her a bell.

'What's this for, *nonna*?' Lola fretted, cupping the bell-hammer with her palm. 'I don't want it! I don't want it!'

'Quiet, child. You must herald the dead.'

We were all there but one; we waited. Jula smoked. Savio didn't come. The four coffin guys stood with their hands clasped in front of them.

'*Mi dispiace*,' said the priest. 'We must proceed. I have to marry a man in Taormina at ten.'

So the men bent their knees and grasped the box handles; Jula did the same. Giosetta faced me then, clutching a posy of white roses.

'Can you get him, Marlena? Can you get Savio? This is impossible! We cannot go without him!'

Her voice cracked, pitiful through her veil.

'OK. Of course.'

So I walked around the back and climbed the outside stairs. Savio's door was ajar; I knocked on it. Getting no answer I pushed on the netting; the door opened into darkness. The blinds were down; I saw him lying there on the bed. I stood on the threshold.

'They're waiting for you,' I said.

I hadn't been back in Savio's room since the day he'd made me clean. Everything was exactly the same. The TV was off; the bed was made. The trophies gleamed behind the polished glass.

'They're waiting,' I said again, taking a small step inside.

He made no reply.

I knew he was awake. I could feel him thinking. He was wearing his black suit. He was lying on his back. He had his hands on his belly and one leg crossed over the other; a white handkerchief covered his face. The deep murmur of the dirge began rising through the house as flies buzzed around his head.

'Savio. Can you hear them? Get up. They're starting. They're waiting for you; they can't go without you. They're waiting for you to carry Analisa.'

It was the most I'd ever said to him. Still he didn't reply. I walked over to him and poked at his shoulder. Then the voice came from under the cotton: 'Analisa was a whore.'

I breathed in and stepped back. He removed the handkerchief to reveal a hideous grin. He repeated: 'Analisa was a whore. And a junkie. And you know something, Marlena? She can wait.'

I looked into his eyes. Dark red rings surrounded them. He had stopped grinning now; he was looking at me very strange. He wasn't blinking; his lips were pursed and twitching.

'Come here, darling,' he said and patted the bed.

'Let's go,' I replied. 'Stop fucking around.'

Then Savio stood up so sudden and so quick that even in July in the heat in my blacks my body turned cold.

He caught me by the wrist. I pulled my arm away so fast my skin burned. He caught me again and pulled me towards him. I kicked at his shin; he slapped me with the back of his hand. He snarled, tore open my dress. With the door wide open and the sun breaking in he hit me again and knocked me down to the floor. I shouted 'No!' He growled; he bit at my breast. In English and Italian now I screamed for Jula to help me, louder as he undid his suit trousers, louder over the dirge – until he grabbed a pillow from the bed and pushed it down on to my face. I couldn't breathe. With my hands I slapped weakly at his head. I heard the flick of his knife. He jabbed in the blade, carving words into the top of my leg. Then he let the knife fall to the floor and he said to me, blood tender: '*Andiamo.*'

The rest is hazy. I was suffocating, delirious now. I remember pain. I remember man-smell on the pillow. Analisa's death-song in my head like hell. And – one, two, three, four: the knell of the funeral bell.

23

Without Savio bearing the weight at front right, the coffin lurched forward as we climbed to the well. It tipped towards Jula. Looking up at it made me trip. My legs were weak from running to catch up; under my dress they buckled and bled. My teeth were rattling; I felt freezing. I was the last in the *cortège*.

I was thinking on my way up that I should never have worn wool. It itched at my skin. It clung to me and made me scratch. I clutched at my own sleeves, I rubbed my legs with my palms; I bit down hard on my hand to try and keep myself still, repeating to myself in a jitter-chatter: 'Analisa was a junkie. Analisa is dead.'

Eventually the taste of blood began to line my mouth. It bubbled at the back of my throat. I had bitten my tongue. When the procession reached the grave-hole dug deep behind the yew patch I knelt down at the row of trees and threw up into the grass.

I don't remember the service. Only the priest saying sing-song that it was her way. I was thirsty; I couldn't swallow. On the way back down with the coffin gone I stopped at the outside tap. I put my mouth up to the metal until my dress and shoes were soaking wet. Jula came to me then; he turned the water off and led me away. He sat with me on the scrub-edge asking questions in the dirt. Then Savio appeared from the crowd.

'I'm so sorry, *mamma*. It was the English girl. She was grabbing at my clothes – look! She wouldn't let me come!'

He showed her his ripped shirt, breathing fast. Then he turned his cheek to reveal a set of nail-scratches on his face.

'She has always wanted something from me – that much has been clear. But to pick such a time, *Mamma*! She must be sick!'

Everyone looked at me. I shivered, palms to the ground. Giosetta came to me then and she lifted her veil.

'You have until nightfall. I want you out.'

Jula took me to Ana's room. He lifted me on to her bed. He rummaged through the drawers; he found a bottle of sleepers and a wad of cotton wool among the pins and spoons. He took my chin and tilted my head; he put a couple of benzos on my tongue. He gave me water. He washed between my legs. He dressed my wounds. He brought my things down from his room and he packed my case.

'What happened?' he kept saying as he helped me to the truck.

'Where are we going?' I garbled. 'Shouldn't you stay with Lo?'

'She'll be all right here for a night. The house'll be heaving with old *signore*. What happened?'

'Where are we going?'

'Jesus, Marlena.'

I climbed into the van. I was almost asleep when he told me: 'We're getting away from here. And then you can talk to me. I'm taking you to the *scala*.'

It was the middle of the night when the sleepers wore off. My thighs were raw and throbbing. My face was covered in sweat. I tried to move – but my body felt like stone. I looked down at myself in the shadows. Jula had taken off all my clothes. I reached down with my hands along my legs; I felt tape and pads of wool. He was lying next to me. The sheets were down around our feet. I didn't remember where we were at first. We were in a single bed.

I looked around me. Thick beams crossed the ceiling. We were at Nikki's. We were up in Lukáš' room. But something was different about it. Lukáš' things weren't there. The wardrobe was open, empty. A few coat hangers hung on the rail. The shelves were bare.

I shuddered. I hate that. I hate it more than anything – you know, when people leave other people and it's as if they were never there. Scanning the room in the darkness I felt like Lukáš had never existed in our lives – like he was dead too. There was no trace of him anywhere. He was gone.

I was still awake thinking about it when Nikki came in. He didn't knock; I didn't speak. I let my eyelids drop to almost shut. He stood wearily at the threshold; I smelled booze and smoke. The hall light flooded in, yellow-white, bright. He came to the foot of the bed. I don't know what he was looking at. Maybe Jula naked. Maybe me, cut. Or maybe it was neither of us. Maybe he was just missing love.

24

When I woke up again Jula was sitting tense-backed on Lukáš' bed. He was dressed. The room was growing light. I lit a half-smoked cigarette.

'You have to tell me what happened,' he said.

I turned on to my side; I winced.

'Do you have any more of Ana's dope?'

'No. You have to tell me.'

'Can you get me some? You must know where.'

'Come on, Marlena. Please.'

So I opened my mouth and shut my eyes; I moved my lips and tongue. I let the words float above my naked body.

'Savio,' I said. 'He raped me.'

Jula stood up. '*L'ho saputo!*'

'The thing is,' I told him. 'I think he did this to someone else.'

'Anželika Pourová – and her mother,' Jula replied – quivering, deliberate, slow.

I sat up, hissing with the pain. 'How do you know about that?'

'The whole of the gypsy community knows about it. Jesus, they've been scouring Catania for months for the guy with the fucking knife!'

He stared at the pads he had taped around my legs.

'Well, they don't need to look any more. Marlena! Now they have found him!'

'The knife's in his room – in a set under his bed,' I said. 'If you need proof. Jula, tell me, what did he write?'

He looked at me pleadingly.

'Don't, Marlena.'

'What does it say? Jula, where are you going?'

His hand rested on the doorknob.

'We don't need proof.'

He beckoned for me to take his hand and stand.

'So where are we going? I want to know what it says! It's only words! How bad can it get? Has he written that I'm a whore?'

I leaned on his arm – then straightened my spine and stood unaided. I pulled my skirt over my smarting thighs.

'No, not that.'

'Then what? Jula!'

He put his head in his hands.

'That you're his,' he said.

He asked if I could walk; I paced the room a while. With Nikki booze-drooling on the couch downstairs, we left by the back door. I didn't ask again where we were going. Jula put my case in the back of the truck. I slept in the van – a sore, troubled sleep. When I awoke I was stiff and cold.

I looked out of my window. The sea was to my left. I saw the blue signs for Catania. Fourteen kilometres. Thirteen, twelve.

We came to the suburbs. In the distance stood the high dock cranes. The city air smelled different to me now; it smelled rotten. I wound up my window. Jula drove through the centre of Catania. It was busy, even at dawn. He went towards the station. Then he headed into the immigrant patch.

'What are you doing?' I cried as he turned on to Via Soreca. 'I don't want to be here! I don't want to see Paolo!'

'We're not here to see him. Stay in the truck. Keep your head down, Marlena. And don't get out.'

I did as he said; I ducked. He stepped into the empty road and looked up at Paolo's flat. But then he walked on; he didn't buzz at 315. Instead he tapped quickly on the shutters of the bar below. A light was on behind them. It seeped into the street. Eventually I heard a noise; someone was rolling up the screens. I peered out over the van door, saw someone short and stocky. Wearing a Hawaiian shirt. Franco.

When Jula came back to the pickup, he was holding something tightly in his right hand. It was wrapped in a glass-cloth; he let it unfold. There, on red chequered muslin. A small black gun.

'What the fuck are you doing with that? Jula, you can't just go and kill!'

'I don't have to,' he answered. 'I'm taking it to the wreck.'

He opened the glove compartment and slid the pistol in.

'You can't do that, you'll be an accessory to murder! And me – I mean, Jula, they'll deport me. They'll kick me out! Can't we just get away from here, leave Sicily? Can't we just take Lola and go?'

He stared ahead; he hadn't heard me. He laughed dryly at a thought I couldn't see.

'There are plenty of people on the site who'd kill him with their bare hands,' he said. 'But with a gun? With this? They can't fail.'

We didn't speak after that. Jula drove down towards the station until he reached *Piazza Giovanni*. There were cars everywhere. He parked. He walked over to the kiosks. I slipped out of the truck. I left a note upon the steering wheel: 'SORRY. GOOD LUCK.'

THREE

The man occupying bed six of the Bari-Geneva sleeper is sallow-skinned and slender; his face is mild and thin. He is sitting there reading just like a puppet – with his head hanging down and his legs dangling over the bunk. He wears brown suit trousers and shiny new brogues; his jacket is off, and hung on a hook. As I slide open the carriage door he looks up all at once from his book. I nod in response and climb the ladder to bed seven, dragging my suitcase behind me.

'*Excuse me*, signorina. *Can I help?*'

He speaks the way a young boy might. He leans curiously towards me, adding: 'Ma non è pesante?'

Pain spears hotly along my shoulders as I twist at the ladder-top to answer his voice. It is a voice full of courtesy and hope.

'*It isn't heavy. It's almost empty. Thank you. No.*'

Once I am up on the bunk I look at the man again. I assess him quickly. He won't do me any harm. He is in his forties. He is handsome – with grey-black hair smoothed back. He is married, too; he pushes his wedding band round his finger the whole time he talks. And he talks, yes, right from the moment we meet; his neat, blackish eyebrows rising

205

and falling as he asks one thing and then another and then he asks again.

'Are you going far?'

'To Como.'

'And you are travelling alone?'

'Yes.'

'You look tired, signorina. Are you ill? And – oh, is that a cut upon your face?'

I shake my hair quick over my cheek.

'Just a scratch. Un graffio – non fa niente. I've had a long day, signore. That's all.'

I take off my coat and with more pain pulsing down my arms and neck I shunt my case on to the overhead rack. I pull the white cotton sleep-sheets over my legs and stare dead ahead. Night is coming. From my bed I can see the platform. I watch the other passengers as they board the train. When the platform is empty and all the carriage doors are slammed shut I see a woman in a uniform lift a green disc above her head. She blows a whistle. The puppet-man heaves out a sigh. We pull out of Bari, the sky spread out like geisha silks. I see church-tops, high-rises, hotels. I see digital clocks with big red numbers showing the temperature and the time. Car factories. Stadiums. Flashing cranes.

Once we are out of the city I kneel up on my bed and pull down the window blind. The man thanks me and tells me he is happy to leave. He says he is going to Milan. I know that already; it is a guidebook he is reading. He thumbs through it as he speaks, peering at the pages in the dim electric light. He is a banker, he tells me. He is going to a conference. There will be other bankers there. Money-men.

'What about you?' he asks. 'What do you do? You look like you could belong in any place. Where have you been?'

'I've just been travelling around. I lived in Sicily. I left there months ago. Today I've come from Brindisi.'

The man frowns like he disapproves.

'You've been travelling? Like a tourist? Brindisi, Madonna! That's not a place to go.'

'I know.'

'But – a tourist – is that what you are?'

'I don't know what I am.'

'Oh,' he replies. 'Oh.'

He puts his book down and he fidgets. He begins to ask me about Sicily. He says that he has never been. He wants to hear of the climate, the sun. Is it hotter than in Rome? Is it easy to find work? He is tired of the way his life is going, tired of money and banks. He has been doing the same thing for more than fifteen years. Do I know how that feels?

In a slow, sleepy drawl I tell him what he wants to know. I say yes, it is hot. Just like anywhere, work isn't hard to find. I tell him the black colour of the Etnean rock and sand. I talk of white-painted buildings, of the orange groves, the women. I speak in Sicilian dialect and make him smile.

'A vita 'ne 'na curuna che ruoda che gira,' I tell him.

'Say it again!' he cries.

Life is a crown that goes turning around. A golden crown turning around and around.

None of what I say to the puppet-man is untrue. I make pictures for him. I don't lie. But I don't tell him how I cut my face, or that I haven't slept, or that I am afraid to try. When I tell the man that my mother was from Burano he gasps out and extends his arm from his top bunk to mine.

'The Venetian lagoons!' he exclaims. 'Che coincidenza! I myself was born in Torcello.'

I bring my arm out from under my sheet and shake his vigorous hand.

'Gianni Clari,' he says. 'Piacere.'

Hours go by. We talk of families. We imagine Venice underwater, sinking. Gianni brings out a plastic box from his

*travelling bag. He pulls out a small brown roll. My stomach
growls at the sight of food. I can't help it – I edge towards
him. He thrusts the sandwich box across the gap at once.*

*'Would you like some?' he asks. 'When was the last time
you ate?'*

'I don't know.'

'Here, take the whole lot. Eat, please. Take it all.'

*My hands shake as I accept the box. I take a roll and I
bite. In a moment it is gone. He urges me to take another. I
push a second roll into my mouth; I am sweating, making
noises. He looks satisfied, shocked. He stares at me. When
the box is empty and I have swallowed my last bite he
offers me water. He unscrews the bottle top.*

'Here, drink.'

I tilt the bottle and gulp. Anxiously he begins to laugh.

'You were hungry,' he says.

'Yes.'

*Then he adds in a quiet voice: 'Signorina, it is not good
to go without food.'*

*For a long time after that we don't speak; the train shoots
through the dark. When we stop at Roma Termini, Gianni
shuffles and coughs. He asks: 'Do you want to come to
Milan?'*

'I don't understand. Milan? What?'

*'It is a three-day stay. My conference. Do you want to
come with me?'*

He pushes his wedding ring round his finger again.

'I'll be staying at the Hotel David.'

'I can't come,' I tell him. 'No.'

*'Forgive me, signorina. I am thinking – well. I'm think-
ing I can feed you. I can pay you. It – it would be company
for me.'*

*He slips the ring off, absent-minded, and shows me his
wallet, flipping it open.*

'I have money! I am a rich man – look!'

He fans out six hundred thousand lire notes. I eye them. They are crisp and new. I think about what he has said, about food set on smart breakfast tables. A place to stay, hot water; clean sheets and a hotel bed.

'You will want for nothing, signorina!'

'I can't,' I tell him again. 'I need to get to Como. There's someone there I need to find.'

Disappointment dulls his eyes; his shoulders droop. He places the notes back in the wallet. I watch them disappear. I feel regret; I reach into my jacket. I have three thousand lire in my pocket, not even enough to buy a pack of cigarettes. I have my photograph too, my battered black and white shot of Jula. And a letter to me, printed in careful red.

'So are you meeting someone at the station?' Gianni whispers meekly. 'Signorina, tell me, what happened to your face?'

'Nothing happened.'

I take off my jacket. He stares and persists.

'Why do you carry an empty case?'

His eyes fix themselves on my mouth. He waits for my answer.

'Because it is all I have.'

A restless silence falls between us in the carriage now. It moves around us. It seems to spin. It is Gianni who breaks it. He pipes: 'Is it a man in Como that you are going to find?'

I don't reply. He asks: 'Do you have a boyfriend there? Un fidanzato?'

'Just someone I used to know,' I tell him as I shake my head.

All the time we are on the train, no conductor ever comes. In the end Gianni stops asking me questions. He chats to me again as if he has never mentioned Milan. I move down into my bed; I grow drowsy. Our conversation

209

dies. Gianni flicks off his reading light and I turn on to my side. It takes me a long time to get to sleep. My body hurts with the rocking train. I keep dreaming and waking. I dream I am standing in an empty piazza. There is a man behind me with a gun. I try to run and can't move. I scream and I am dumb. But it is never real; each time I groan and lurch upright there is only Gianni. Smiling benevolent, alert – like a brother might smile. There in the moving shadows. Willing me to rest.

When I wake again it is to the sound of female voices. French voices in the carriage. I open my eyes and look down. Two nuns are arranging their belongings on the bottom bunks. The man Gianni Clari is gone. One of the nuns pulls on the blind-cord; the carriage fills with greenish light. She opens the sash window with a grunt. The air smells clean and cold. I sit up in my bunk and pull off the sheets.

'What time is it?' I ask her in Italian. 'Have we reached Como? Excuse me, please – but did we pass Milan?'

She doesn't understand. I tap my wrist. She shows me her watch: half past six in the morning. Como is our next stop. I swing my legs down off the bed; my body aches. Something digs at my back. I reach with my hand and fumble; tucked under my pillow is Gianni's guide. I open it and flick through it. I gape at the book. The nuns bustle in their thick, brown habits, babbling to each other in their language. I whisper to myself, amazed, in mine. For in the guide, under the sharp, wide-angle shot of the Hotel David, are the words: 'IN CASE YOU CHANGE YOUR MIND!'

The page itself is marked with three brand new hundred thousand lire notes.

I

The markets were running on *Piazza Giovanni* the morning I left Catania. We were blessed, Jula mumbled to himself as we left Franco's bar with the gun. Driving down in the direction of the station, we found the streets bottlenecked. The main junction was jammed. We stopped short of the kiosks and parked. The *piazza* was filled with vendors and vans.

Jula climbed out quick, taking the gun wrapped in its glass-cloth. He didn't speak to me. He didn't look back. Through the open window of the truck I heard the first market chants of the morning; a few women were already shouting hellos to one another as they wandered from pitch to pitch. And there were kids everywhere: Sicilian and African boys scuttling around, helping to unload. It was fortunate; it was fate. It was good that there was a crowd.

Some of the kids were raising the stalls. They crouched in pairs under long metal tables, fixed them together with brackets and bolts. Others clambered into the backs of the vans, hauling out crates crammed with fresh stock: figs, bread, mandarins, whole swordfish laid on ice; picture frames, posters, island maps, vats of olive oil, vinegar, wine. I felt weak. My stomach hurt. I watched the kids scuttling with their bottles and boxes, dance-dodging Jula as he moved through the crowd. Some of them knew him.

They called his name: '*Ciao, Jula! Cosa fai così presto?*
Dove vai?'

I watched him as he pushed his way down the narrow
gaps between the vans and the stalls – until he reached the
station kiosks where the Roma stood.

I wrote my good luck note with one of Lola's broken cra-
yons. Then I opened the pickup door. Sucking in the dawn
air through my teeth, I tried to stand. I slumped against
the truck, clutching the wing-mirror; I knocked my head on
the metal frame. People bustled round me. I steadied myself, tried again. I fixed my gaze on the vapour-trails criss-
crossing the sky; I counted the early planes. By the time I
managed to stand alone Jula had disappeared from view.

I stumbled across the *piazza*. More crowds were moving in. Women walked arm in arm, jostling me. I came to a
bench. With my legs shaking I climbed on to the slats. I
had a good view from there; I could see the station steps.
I could see Jula. He was at one of the coffee stands. He
was standing in a ring of Romany men – his hair in his
eyes and his hands raised up. He was talking, shouting. He
looked just like them. I watched as a tall guy in a red
checked coat stooped on the steps and locked his arms
around Jula. Then my view was blocked. A fat woman in a
bright pink dress was waving her bag in front of my face.

'These seats are not for standing on, *signorina*! You
make them dirty with your shoes!'

'Of course,' I said, leaning forward.

Red checks, raised hands. I saw him again. The woman
dabbed her forehead with a handkerchief edged with roses.

'*Well?*' she demanded. 'Do you want me to call the
warden, *signorina*?'

Jula pushed the gun-bundle on to the checked man's chest.
Then it was gone, thrust into an inside pocket. The man
kissed Jula on the face. Blood rushed to my fingers and

lips; the pain in my legs seemed to vanish. I lurched down off the bench, half-running; I trampled a geranium bed to get to the street. The pink woman shrieked.

'*Umbriaca! Straniera!*'

She spat on her handkerchief and began cleaning the slats; she watched me stagger over the road to where the coaches ran.

At the only booth open, I bought a one-way ticket to Messina. A man in a suit smiled at me behind mirror sunglasses and shoved my suitcase into the hold. He punched a hole in my ticket. With a click of his fingers he ushered me on. The steps were steep. I boarded slow. I pulled myself up with the rail and wandered to the back.

By the time I reached the seat at the fire-exit door, my chest was throbbing, my hands were trembling. My throat was sore and dry. From there I could see all the way across the markets. I tried to catch sight of Jula through the glass. Then the coach engine started. The TV came on. The air conditioning blew cold air and dust. *Ladies and Gentlemen this is the 640 airport service to Messina. Today we will call at Catania Fontanarossa, Monte Tesoro, Acireale, Fiumefreddo, Giardini-Naxos and Messina Port. Anyone who does not desire to travel should leave the vehicle at once. Please keep your bags out of the aisle. Have a pleasant journey. Thank you.*

It turned out the interchange for Fontanarossa was just a few kilometres beyond Monte Tesoro. It backed right on to the chemical plant; only an ill-coloured stream and a rusting fence divided the two pieces of land. It was a small terminal; it had three bays. Next to the ticket office was a tiny bar. I had never even known it existed – although, thinking about it then, as I stared through the window into the stream's oily green, it made sense to me. I had known a few bus drivers at Mickeys; they would stroll into the club after the late night run, removing their ID badges from their work shirts as they ordered a drink and scanned the booths for a girl.

When we stopped at the terminal the driver with the mirror shades got out. The doors puffed open; at once the stink from the factory filled the bus. I covered my mouth and nose with my jacket collar. I saw a second driver step out from the bar. I watched him; he was smoking. I thought maybe I knew him from the club. He said a few words to the mirror guy – then he stubbed out his cigarette and took the ticket punch and keys. He boarded the bus; he stood at the aisle-end under the TV and took off his coat. I recognized him for sure now in his short, white sleeves – by the blue dragon tattoo that coiled down from his elbow to his wrist. The dragon-tail twisted as he rubbed his hands together, ready to start his shift. He threw his coat up on to the seat behind him and got behind the wheel.

The only other passengers who boarded at Monte Tesoro were a bunch of teenage kids – all thin and pale and wearing black. There were four of them: three guys and a girl. They all wore black lipstick. They gangled up the aisle, almost to the back. When they saw me hunched at the fire-exit door they retreated; they crossed to the other side. There they sprawled on to the seats, hanging over the backs of them, passing around a Walkman and talking about some death metal band; then they started laughing and holding their noses because of the chemical plant's bad smell.

I looked back at the factory chimney and its line of thick smoke. The coach started up and we pulled out of the bay. I was glad to be moving – but then as we turned on to the road the bus suddenly stopped again. I sat up in my seat and craned my neck. The grunge kids peered forward to see. Someone was standing in the middle of the street, right in front of the bus. It was a girl; she was waving her hand. The driver opened his window and shouted: '*Ma sei pazza o che cosa? Che cazzo stai facendo? Tutt'a posto? Cosa fai?*'

He knew her. I could tell from the soft way he cursed her. I didn't catch what it was she said back. She boarded quickly. She had no ticket. It didn't matter. The dragon guy restarted the bus. The girl sat down on the very front seat of the coach and hugged the bag she had placed in her lap.

'*Ma che fai?*' the driver asked again. 'Where are you going? What the fuck were you doing, jumping out in front of my bus?'

She laughed anxiously and began to talk. Over my seat I could see the top of her head; her straight, shiny hair, her small, tense back. Above the engine I heard the trails and traces of her faint, flustered voice as she offered her story to the driver. I knew her too. It was Carme.

The whole time I was living out in Monte Tesoro, Carme never left Catania. It was like she never even dared think of it. Blasto took her everywhere. So I knew something was wrong when she boarded the coach. When we stopped in Giardini-Naxos she hurried down the steps with her eyes full of tears like she wanted to go back home. She paced up and down by the coach side. Sometimes she came right up to the fire door where I was sitting and stood below it, tap-tapping her feet. She was directly beneath me; I could see her close. She wore a white coat with a fake fur collar; she had a gold clip in her hair. She didn't look up; she just stood there, tapping and clutching her phone. When it started to rain she came back inside. She took off her coat and sat down. I got up then and pushed open the windows. I smelled the town, the sea, the rain – all wafting in. Still drowsy from the painkillers Jula had given me, I stretched my legs out along the back seat and closed my eyes. I tried to think of everything that had happened, get it in order – but I couldn't. So I counted my breath until I fell asleep.

When I woke up the bus had stopped. We were parked on Messina harbour. I looked down the length of the coach. The driver was still behind the wheel. He was reading a book. I could see his back, his arms; his blue tattoo. I glanced around me. Everyone else was gone. The grunge kids and Carme had taken their cases; in the distance I could see them filing on to a bridge that led from the dock on to the deck of a big white boat. I got up and ran down the aisle, mumbling to myself, half-tripping down the exit steps. I was wasted with pain and confusion and too little sleep.

'You okay?' said the dragon guy, raising his eyes from his page.

I mouthed a silent yes. I walked along the side of the bus. The hold was open. It was dark and empty. I had to fight the impulse not to crawl in there and lie down. The guy came down on to the steps and said: 'Hey, don't I know you from somewhere? Don't you work down at Mickeys? In the club?'

'I used to,' I told him.

'You sure you're all right?'

I reached in and took my case.

Green limpet-covered walls, white water-marks on the docks. *La Madonna Della Lettera* open-armed in the rain. Violet clouds rolling down from the hills. These are the things I remember about leaving Sicily. The summer seemed suddenly gone. I walked on to the ferry deck, watched the passengers playing one-armed bandits and drinking at the bar. I sat on the wet plastic chairs and looked back. I smoked a couple of cigarettes, watched the signs for CAMPARI and MARTINI flashing weakly on the building sides. I looked even when they had gone, when Messina was no more than a change in colour on the Sicilian horizon, a blur on the top of the sea.

At Villa San Giovanni, a second footbridge was let down. I left the deck then; I shuffled along with the crowd of foot passengers who stood waiting behind a chain. I saw Carme again. As the stewards let the chain drop and the people began to cross, I weaved and pushed to get close to her. I reached her; I placed my hand on her shoulder. She turned to me, startled. Her nose was newly broken, swollen at the bone. When she saw who I was she gasped and cupped her hands quickly around the break.

'Oh! Marlena!'

'Where are you going?' I asked her.

'I'm going to Brindisi! I met a man who can find me work there. Pippo. He . . . he's meeting me the other end!'

I lowered my voice.

'Did Blasto do that to you?'

She whimpered and brought her hands down. Dark blood caked her nostrils. She didn't answer my question. She just squeaked defeatedly: 'What about you?'

'I'm leaving,' I said. 'I don't know where I'm going. Christ, Carme, that looks really sore.'

'Do you – do you need a job?'

My response was automatic.

'Sure. Do you think your Pippo will have enough work for two?'

'I don't know.'

Carme gave me the flicker of a smile and her eyes smarted from the pain.

'Maybe. But come anyway! I can't face the world alone!'

I nodded. I was glad of the distraction. We passed the stewards; she walked in front of me. Below us the water looked black and cold – and a long way down. At the final section of the bridge Carme's heel got caught and she stumbled. She let out a little cry; she reached for the rail. With my back finally turned on Sicily, and with the tenderness of a new suitor, I slipped my arm around her waist to steady her as we stepped on to land.

2

No Pippo ever turned up to meet Carme from her train. We waited for over two hours. He never came. We went and sat up on the station wall, by the phone box at the cab ranks – where he had told her to be. Together we scanned the crowds, Carme gazing needily into the face of every man who approached the taxi queue. But none of them stopped for her. None was Pippo. They were just ordinary Italian Friday-night guys, coming into Brindisi from the suburbs to drink and then go home.

'He's not coming,' I said eventually.

I lit a half-cigarette from my coat. The stone underneath me had turned cold and damp. Above the city lights the evening sky was a blackish blue.

'How do you know this guy anyway?' I asked her.

'Oh, I met him on the net.'

She chewed at her nails with frenzied teeth and twittered: 'I just don't understand why he's not here! He was sure to be, that's what he said. Just wait by the taxis – at the top end, on the wall! He said we would go back to his place. He said he'd feed me and give me my keys and my kit!'

'What kit?' I asked.

Carme's eyes danced about, aloof, in her head.

'I told you, I wouldn't be a table girl for ever, Marlena! My uniform! My strippogram kit!'

'Jesus, Carme,' I said, trying to imagine myself in a nurse's paper hat. I let out a dry laugh. 'You never said anything about strippograms.'

'Well, it's better than what – *you* do! And to think, I sent him the fee!'

'What fee?'

'The introduction fee – the money for the clothes.'

'How much? Did you send it to his house?'

'No, to his postal box. Fifty thousand lire!'

I sat and slid down off the wall, my legs stinging, wet dirt smearing on my palms.

'Come on Carme,' I said. 'Let's go. We need to find somewhere to stay.'

Halfway into town in a jeweller's shop doorway we counted the money we had. It started raining again. Carme kept saying she was cold. She kept jerking up on to her tiptoes and shivering. She started snivelling and checking her phone.

'How will we manage, on our own? Without work?' she whined.

Her voice was full of tears. I held out the notes in front of her.

'It's OK. Look. I think we have enough for a room.'

She followed me to a tobacco kiosk like a child follows its mother. I bought an evening paper and a map of the town. I pored over the ads under the kiosk light. I called a few numbers up. Most places we couldn't afford. The only room we had the money for was above a Turkish bar. The guy on the phone said it was small. It was meant for one.

'But you can share it, *signorina*!' I heard the Arab in his voice as it came crackling down the line. 'It's to the west of town. Along the dock road – after the railway bridge. About three kilometres. On the corner of Via Di Grecia! You should find it without trouble, *insh'allah*!'

We walked there together in the cutting rain.

The place was called Bar Barakas. The guy was right – it was pretty easy to find. But it turned out it wasn't a bar at all. It was some kind of smoking café. It had bamboo blinds rolled all the way down the windows and door – so you couldn't tell what was in there, your sight was blocked by lines of orange light. I turned the handle. I heard the jangling of an old-fashioned bell. Carme and I stepped into a room full of Arab men. The air was sweet with hookah smoke. The men lay on couches, playing chess and cards. They stared at us, at our wet clothes and hair. They clicked their tongues. A man with a moustache leaned over his table and pursed his lips in a kiss.

'I don't like it here,' Carme whinged. 'Marlena, I want to go.'

I took her arm and I led her across the floor to a food counter made of glass. She leaned against it, hopeless, looking in at the food. There were raw kebabs on one side and cakes on the other. I called over to a man who was making coffee. He was steaming milk.

'Excuse me,' I said. 'The room?'

He turned around. He was slim; he wore glasses. He had a waiter's apron on and a red cravat. He smiled very wide. I saw the pink of his gums. He poured hot milk into a half-filled coffee glass.

'Two girls in the room for the price of one?' He laughed at the joke and I glimpsed his gums again. 'You are lucky, eh? I give you special deal. One minute. Yes, yes.'

He came out from behind the counter and took the coffee to the pursing man. The way he moved was graceful. He seemed to glide across the floor. Then he came back to us and shook our hands. He said his name was Abdesalam. He led us through a door at the side of the counter. The room was on the first floor.

It was nothing much. I mean, it was what I expected. It had a sink and a single bed. It looked over the back of the café. The guy flicked the light switch; the bulb flashed on for a second and then blew. He gave a little shout of surprise and hurried away, back down the stairs. Carme and I stood together in the dark.

'I don't like it here,' she said to me again. 'I'm hungry. I want to go home.'

'Don't be dumb,' I told her.

'I mean it! I want to go back!'

The man reappeared. He had a new bulb in his hand. He reached up and took the blown one out then screwed the other in. In the new, yellow light I saw the walls were peeling. There were no shutters or blinds. The window was open, jammed. Rain had come in on to the floor and the head of the bed. I walked in, looked down on to the street, on to a pile of rubbish bags. Then I backed into the hall; I stuck my head around another open door. It was a toilet, a hole in the floor. The guy Abdesalam followed me and asked: 'So you want it?'

'Yes.'

'Okay. You pay now.'

We went back into the room; Carme was sitting on the bed.

'You want another night, you pay in the morning. Sorry, there is no key.'

'No key for the room?' Carme repeated with a wail, as I counted out damp notes and gave them to him.

'No, the lock is broken. There was some fighting here,' he said. 'What happened to your nose?' he asked Carme gummily, as he closed the door and jiggled the lock fitting to show us it was loose. 'Please don't bring trouble here, ladies. I am a peaceful man.'

Once the man had gone back downstairs Carme began to cry.

'Oh, this is awful!' she sniffed. 'This is terrible! I hate it here! How will we pay him again?'

I looked at her. Tears were running down her cheeks. Her nose was beginning to bleed. I pulled some cotton wool from my bag, from the stuff Jula had given me. I handed it to her. She dabbed pathetically at the blood.

'I can get money,' I said.

'Oh, I want to see Blasto!'

'You can't go back to him, Carme.'

'That's easy for you to say!'

Blood and tears pooled on her top lip; they dripped on to her coat. They made shapes like flowers on her collar. She started shivering again. I could hear her teeth chattering; I leaned over her. I took her clothes off. I let my wet hair down and tied hers up with the band. Naked like that I could see the brown and yellow bruises that covered Carme's chest and arms. She climbed under the sheets, still sobbing, not caring what I had seen. I knelt at the side of the bed.

'You can't go back to him,' I said again.

I took her hands in mine and I held them until she fell asleep.

Once Carme's breathing had deepened I let go of her hands. I took my own wet clothes off now and slung them up on the curtain rail. I peeled the dressings from my legs. My wounds were angry, stinging red. I opened my case. I pulled on a pair of tights. I put on a skirt and a tiger print top. I put on lipstick. I took my coat. Then I walked back down the stairs. The café was emptier now. The pursing

223

man stood up and smiled. He walked over to me as I headed for the door. His voice was slow and gluey; his breath smelled of coffee. He said: 'My wife is an old mare. I want a woman who can move like a mamba!'

Then he laughed very deep and long.

'Is that you?' he asked.

I thought of what the guy Abdesalam had said.

'No,' I told him, as I opened the door and stepped out into the rain. The bell jangled as I pulled it shut.

Once on the street I doubled back towards the station. I went down on to the dock road; I heard the rumble of the sea. The rain was hard that night; it was cold. I saw no other girls around. I stopped when I reached the shelter of the overpass. There I opened my coat and faced the traffic, waiting for the first car to stop under the bridge; to flash and to slow.

3

The next morning I awoke to the sound of Carme's troubled breath. I opened my eyes; she was on her back. Her mouth was hanging open. The pillow we had shared was spotted with patches of dried blood. I said her name; she rolled on to her side with a snort. Her nose was more swollen than the night before. Her eyes had come up black. She opened them like a frightened puppy and let out a yelp, bringing her hands up to the break.

'Ow, I can't breathe! It hurts, Marlena!'

I sat up, my back to her now. My bare feet touched the cold floor. I was sore, much worse than yesterday. It hurt to stand. In the unfamiliar shadows I pulled on my clothes with half my usual speed.

'Here, I got you these,' I said to Carme, once I had dressed.

I threw a pack of *madeleine* on to the end of the bed. She sat up and wrapped the sheets around her. She opened the pack.

'We should go to the hospital,' I told her.

Carme nodded, her mouth full of cake.

'They won't ask who did it, will they?'

'You don't have to say.'

'How will we get there? What will they do to me? Ow, Marlena, it hurts to chew!'

'They'll give you painkillers. Then it won't hurt. You'll

have to ask for strong ones. You'll have to tell them how much pain you're in.'

I looked through her bag and got her out some dry clothes. Then I went down to the café and waited for her there. I drank an espresso. I paid the guy Abdesalam for a second night. Then with the rest of the money I had made down on the docks Carme and I took a taxi to the south side of town.

I don't like hospitals. They give me the creeps. All that striplight and smell of sickness. All that waiting in sterile air. The walk-in place was in the basement. Everything down there was painted green. We had to queue up at a little green hatch. Carme hid behind me as I gave her name.

'Carmela Verga,' I said to the receptionist. 'Her nose is broken.'

'*Va bene*, someone will come for you. Please sit down.'

So we sat down together on a row of cold metal chairs and flicked through beauty magazines. It was almost an hour later when a nurse with black hair that was scraped up into a bun came and screeched Carme's name.

'*Carmela Verga!*'

We both stood up. The nurse scratched something down on her clipboard and clacked ahead of us. We followed her down pale green corridors. They stank of antiseptic. We went through some swinging glass doors and turned at a sign on the wall that read: EARS NOSES THROATS.

The bun left us there, at another row of chairs. We sat down again. We watched a TV that was fixed to the wall. It was some chat show all about how to keep your man. A doctor came. He wore a long white coat. He had a voice like milk: smooth and warm. He had a young boy with him, wearing a jacket and tie.

'I have a student here with me today,' said the doctor. 'Do you mind if he sits in?'

The boy smiled, benign. Carme shook her head.

We walked into a large square room. Carme was asked to sit on a leather chair. The doctor leaned on one of the arms and bent his knees. He looked up Carme's nose with a little black torch. Then he sprayed something from a can into both her nostrils. He put a mirror to her face. He asked her how much it would trouble her to have a nose that was no longer straight. It was quite a bad break, he said. But then again, he had seen worse. Carme was unsure. She looked at me.

'I can reset it,' said the doctor. 'But it will mean a few injections. Why don't you go and get yourselves a drink? I have another patient I can see while you decide. Take some time to think.'

We left the room and sat back down in front of the TV. The show host was saying the key to keeping your man was PAPA: Patience, Acceptance, Praise and Appearance.

'I hate needles,' Carme said to me, her bottom lip quivering. 'I don't want to have it done.'

'PAPA!' exclaimed the TV host into her microphone.

Some guy from the audience took the mike and told her that was a load of crap.

'I think the break is pretty,' I told Carme. 'Better, even. I do.'

She looked at me like I was crazy. She took out her phone.

'I'll be back in a minute,' she mumbled.

She got up quick. She disappeared around a corner. I didn't go after her. I sat and watched the rest of the show. By the time she reappeared it had finished. Everyone was clapping and waving into the camera eye.

'Marlena?'

Carme stood in front of me and smiled feebly as she said: 'I've changed my mind. He thinks I should have it done.'

Carme cried so much when the doctor reset her nose that he left us alone in his room after he was finished.

'I'll give you a minute,' he said as he peeled off his rubber gloves.

The student boy followed him.

'It's OK,' I said to her, as she lay on the bed. 'It's done. They've gone now.'

But she kept her eyes screwed shut, like someone was still hurting her. Tears ran down her temples on to her hair. I looked around the room. I bent down and opened a cabinet below the main sink. There were dressings in there, boxes of antiseptic wipes. I took them. I stuffed them into my bag. Carme sat up.

'What are you doing? I won't need those, will I?'

'Maybe. Come on. Let's go.'

As we left the doctor handed Carme a prescription and smiled at her kindly. At the sight of him she burst into tears again and flounced out of the room. I didn't follow her. I stopped at the threshold where he stood. He smiled a second time.

'I don't make many friends,' he said, all milky and real. He undid his coat and sat back down at his desk. 'Why should I? After all, it is only the pulse of the pain that I feel.'

I stood in the doorway not moving.

'*Signorina*, are you all right?

'I'm fine,' I told him. 'The pulse?'

He didn't answer.

'You look as if you have suffered a trauma? You are the victim of the attack too?'

It was funny, the way he said the words. *Tra-u-ma*. *At-tack*. He made them sound like music.

'No,' I told him. 'No.'

'Ah, well. Sometimes I get it wrong. The pulse, yes; only the pulse, *signorina*. Never the pain itself.'

Back at Barakas, once Carme was asleep, I took a couple of her painkillers. I sat on the end of the bed and ate the rest of the *madaleine*. Then I changed my clothes and left the café. I went back down on the docks, did a couple of handjobs. One guy took me west, to his flat.

When I got back it was late. The mamba guy was there. He got up from his seat and lowered his head as I came in, some kind of twisted courtesy. I didn't look. He followed me across the floor and through to the stairs. Behind the door he jeered: 'So? You are all alone?'

I didn't understand him.

'Paying double rent!'

Still I didn't stop. He grabbed my ankle. He had long fingernails. They dug into my skin. He stuck out his tongue and let it ripple pale pink in front of me.

'I want to buy you!' he spluttered.

I kicked my leg free. I ran up the stairs. I looked down to see him looking up, puckering his brown lips, his tongue back in his mouth. I went into the room and turned on the light. I barricaded the door with the bed. And I understood what he had said now: that I was all alone. Carme was gone.

4

On a coverless pillow damp with rain and stained with tiny patches of Carme's blood, I fell asleep. I slept for what seemed like a long time. I had a dream. I dreamed that I was walking in an empty town. It was daytime; it was Sicily, but there was no sun. The sky was pale and overcast. The streets were dull. I passed a row of shops, all with their shutters down. All of them closed except for one. It was a small clothes shop. It had mannequins standing in the window. A sign hung on chains over the door. The sign was square and white and made of wood. It had the word BOUTIQUE written on it in slanted gold.

I stopped at the open shop. I looked in through the window. The mannequins had flowers in their hair. They were dressed in dancing clothes. They wore sequinned blue bikinis and matching gloves. They had their feet stepping forward and their hands on their hips. They were in symmetry with one another. At least, that was how it seemed. One of the mannequins had bleached hair. The other was a strawberry blonde.

I stepped closer to the glass and tapped on it. Suddenly the yellow-haired mannequin moved with a start. It was Carme. She knocked her arm against the window. It came off at the elbow. She jerked down to look. It had fallen at her feet. She stared at it, opening her plastic mouth. She cried out. It was a hollow sound.

'Carme?' I said, dream-slow. 'Is that you?'

She knelt in the shopfront and looked at me very guarded. She didn't trust me. She picked up the broken arm. Then she stumbled down from the platform, leaving the other mannequin standing there.

'Carme?' I repeated as she stepped outside.

She lifted up the section of arm, like she was showing it to me. Jutting out from it was a bolt.

'Where are you going?' I shouted, as she edged away on her plastic feet. She began to half-run, fake flowers dropping from her hair.

'I'm going back! I can't do it, Marlena! I have to go back!'

Once Carme was out of sight I turned to face the shop window again. The other mannequin was perfect. She was beautiful. She was still. She didn't step down. She just stood there in her catwalk pose. I stared at her. She was intact.

'Hello,' I mouthed.

She didn't move. She gave no signs of life. It was only as I turned and stepped back into the road that I thought I saw her stir. I looked back at her over my shoulder. Her position had changed. She had come closer to the glass. Like she was swearing her survival under oath, she had raised her hand. In her image I raised my own. Then she was motionless again. Only a price tag – one hundred thousand lire – dangled from her glove.

When I awoke from the dream I sat cross-legged on the floor of the room and wrote a letter on the back of a cigarette packet.

Jula,
I hope this gets to you. Maybe you are already gone. I am in Brindisi. I am working here. I can save money – if the winter is not too hard. Where are you? I could come to you.
Marlena

I pulled my jacket from the bed and searched in the inside pocket. I found my black and white print. I took it from its envelope. I pushed the note into the envelope and put the picture back. Then I wrote on the front:

JULA SCHIGGHIAPEDDI
Presso FERMO POSTA
MOTTA CAMASTRA
SICILIA

I stared at what I had written, at the look of Jula's name. I licked the envelope. I tasted gum on my tongue. Then I took the pen and added on the back:

MARLENA LUPONE
Presso BAR BARAKAS
VIA GRECIA 77
BRINDISI

5

By the time the autumn came – with its strange, green skies and weeks of rain – my wounds had healed over. The pain from them had gone. They still looked ugly, for sure; my scars were a deep, violent red. But the skin didn't break any more or weep when I walked the dock road. I no longer bled.

Not that I got much business. The regular Brindisi girls would hiss me off the strip. I had to go right down to the far end of the beat, the black end. *La Statale Nera*: that was what everyone called it. The stretch where the Moroccan and Tunisian girls stood. The African girls were all right. They didn't talk to me all that much. But they left me alone. They didn't hiss. Sometimes on the slow nights they would saunter over and say hello. I was no threat to them. The punters who drove on to *La Statale* wanted black skin, not white.

Eventually I went back to the railway bridge. It was filthy in there, tar-dark. It stank of seagull shit. No one talked to you on that part of the beat. Only the clippers and the crack-heads worked it. No one cared in there. No one said hello. If a girl got beaten up the chances were she'd been picked up in the tunnel. It was the cheapest beat in Brindisi, even cheaper than *La Statale*. Under the bridge the price of a fuck was ten thousand lire.

In the end I got sick of it, working for nothing. I had trouble two shifts in a row. Some guy punched me in the mouth for getting his name wrong. He split my lip and broke one of my teeth. Then the next night these two Turkish guys robbed me and dumped me on the outskirts of town. I quit the streets then. I went instead to the sailors' bars. I even waited by the ships sometimes, moored and lit up at the quay – and when the harbour was empty I tried the city clubs, dressing my best.

Sometimes I could get to the end of the night and have made no cash at all. I couldn't pay my next day's rent. I couldn't eat. On those nights I would crawl back to my room, disheartened, cold. Unable to sleep I would write more letters to the farm. *Jula, sometimes I think of you. Jula, I think of coming back. Jula, let me know if you get this. Jula, where are you now?* I imagined my letters to him travelling in a sack on the Circumetnea train. They felt like the first letters of my life. Months went by. I imagined them waiting for him in a pile at the post office in Motta Camastra. I imagined Jula disappeared, arrested, dead. I imagined Giosetta taking the bundle of letters in a bundle and burning them on the fire. I spent a whole winter in that room, saving nothing, counting days.

With the end of winter came a trickle of tourists – backpackers filing through Brindisi on their way over to the warmth of Greece. Tourist men all look the same to me. They travel in groups. They like to get drunk. When I could get them to buy me, they paid better than the sailors; I could pretty much charge them anything – they had no idea. So as the rains ended and the air turned dry, I trawled the clubs and hotels, working each place a couple of nights and then moving on. I didn't want to get myself kicked out of anywhere. I hate that. There's always such a scene. But no one seemed to notice what I was doing. I can make myself look like a tourist too. It's easy. All you need is a pair of shorts and sunglasses. All you need to do is act dumb.

It was one night early in March when I met these two guys from Washington. They were on their way back from Corfu. They were a funny pair – one of them was big and loud. He talked a lot; he was broad and tanned. He wore a hockey hat. His name was Bill. The other guy was short and quiet; he had ginger hair and large bright freckles dotted all over his face. Anyway, they caught my eye in this bar I was in and the guy Bill shouted me over to their table.

'Been stood up?' he bellowed, slapping an empty chair with his hand.

I sat down. The guys told me they were students. Biology and botanics was what they said. Bill bought me whiskies and urged me to slam them as he wound my hair around his thick, brown fingers and stroked my arms. The redhead sat there drinking banana creams. They had money to burn, Bill said. He and his buddy were at the end of their trip. Tomorrow they would return to the American east coast.

'How long you been away from the UK?' Bill asked, wiping his mouth with his forearm. 'You a student too?'

'No.'

'But you've been to Greece, right? Did you get along to the Athens festivals? Listen, what are doing later on? You want to come back to our rooms with us? We got plenty more beer.'

'Sure, I'll come,' I said.

He squeezed at my arm.

'What I mean is, I'll come if you can pay me.'

The guy's mouth flopped open for a second. Then he shut it and pulled like a kid at the peak of his cap.

'W-w-w-wow, man, are you serious?' he stuttered, his face flushing with a mix of delight and dismay.

He looked over at his friend in disbelief. The redhead sucked on his straw and shrugged. Bill looked back at me.

He laughed and took his hat off and put it on his knees and said in a tepid voice: 'Hell, I might as well. Hell, yeah. It's party time!'

So I followed them out of the bar. We got in a taxi. The redhead sat in the front. Bill and I sat next to one another in the back. It was funny: he didn't speak to me or touch me on our journey; he just stared out of the window at the city lights as the cab cruised along late-night streets, taking us to the wealthy side of town. The guys were staying in an apartment; it belonged to some American aunt or other. It was in a complex; it had a pool and an electric gate. It had a rose garden and a patio with chairs and chequered stones. Bill punched in the gate code and we crunched up a gravel drive. We sat out on the patio for a while, under one of those round outdoor heaters. Bill opened a bottle of Greek *ouzo*. He kept asking me questions, snapping them at me. Where had I lived in my life? Where was I born? He leaned over the table, frowning, stiff.

'I don't get it,' he said, finally. 'Are you a druggie or something? Why do you do this? Why?'

When he asked that the redhead got up and went to his room. He flashed me an apologetic smile. Bill folded his arms and turned away. I watched the side of his face, the blue light coming up from the pool. His mouth was slightly open, another question forming on his lips. I had no answers for him. I decided I should go. I stood up to leave and it was then that he spoke again. He beckoned me with reluctant hands, his voice decisive, flat: 'Okay. C'mon.'

Then this weird thing happened. I had never had a walk-out before. Bill led me into the flat; it smelled of new paint. We went into the bedroom. He took off his clothes and lay on the bed. I took off my dress. He said: 'So, I never went with a whore before. What's the deal?'

I glanced round the room for objects; he was making me nervous. Ashtray. Lamp.

'Well, you just tell me what you want.'

'I don't know what I fucking want!'

He raised his hands behind his head.

'I thought you were just some cute girl in a bar. I didn't figure you were a hookèr,' he said.

I didn't want to wait around. I took a chance. I reached out to touch him, kneeling on the bed. He sprang back in disgust; he pulled a sheet over his body.

'Don't do that,' he told me.

'Maybe I should go,' I said, standing up at the bedside. 'This is a waste of time.'

'You're telling me!' he cried. He sat up now, pointing. 'I mean, Christ, what the hell are those horrible marks?' He was pointing between my legs. I pulled on my dress and covered the scars. 'How can you let yourself get all fucked up like that?'

I picked up my bag. His voice softened, unexpected.

'Look, I'm sorry, man. Why don't you stay and talk to me?'

I walked to the door. Bill stood up and reached on the floor for his jeans; he rummaged in the pockets and handed me my fee.

'Here. Here, take it. C'mon, stay and talk to me.'

But it was too late; his voice was making me angry. His words were rattling around in my head. I punched him on the hand. He let go of the money and it fell. I left him crouching there, naked, picking up dollars.

Outside, the garden was empty. I walked the length of the pool. Once I got beyond the light from the water I sat down on the patio stones. I smelled chlorine and roses. I took out my mobile. I ordered myself a cab. Then, for the first time since I left Sicily, I called the farm. I pressed in the numbers one after the other. My hands were trembling, cold. Regret coursed through my veins. I heard the ghost of Jula's voice in my head. Then I buried my face in my hands. The line was dead.

6

'**M**arlena Anna Lupone?'

My name was sung in a taunt from behind the broken door. I didn't have to open it to know who it was. That slow, sticky voice. It was the mamba man. He knocked and said the name again. He stepped into the room. I scowled at him.

'Go away.'

I was sitting on the bed. I was counting up money, trying to scrape up a rent. He paid no attention. He didn't leave. He just stood there, his eyes very round and black. He bent towards me, his hands behind his back. The hairs on my arms all stood on end as he put his tongue out and with the tip of it he licked his black moustache.

'What do you want?' I shuddered. 'Who told you my name?'

He closed his eyes and began to chuckle. I shuffled down the bed.

'I have something for you,' he gloated, sidling towards me.

My voice surfaced, breaking and thin: 'Oh?'

He knelt before me. He brought his arms from behind his back. He had a letter. My name on the front in neat red capitals. I reached forward to grab it. The man snatched it back.

'Where did you get it? How long have you had it?' I cried.

'*Importante?*' he breathed, waving it in the air.

'Give it to me!'

He slid the letter into his breast pocket.

'You bastard! Give it back!'

'No. It is mine. But like I said, my wife no longer pleases me. Come on, *signorina*, think about it. Maybe now my price is right?'

I eyed the letter jutting out of his pocket, the cream-coloured envelope, the red edge of the stamp. I had to have it. I had to read it.

'OK,' I said.

He was disarmed at the speed of the bargain. He let out a victorious laugh. Then a look of greed set in his face and he unzipped his trousers, pulled down his pants. He smelled sour, like he hadn't washed in days. I lifted my skirt. I held on to the bed frame and looked to the ceiling as I hooked my legs around his back.

'Move, girl!' he panted as I hooked my legs around his back – so I made my body ripple back and forth just like a basket snake.

I thought only of the letter. He grabbed my head, poked his tongue into my mouth and ears. He ranted in Arabic, gobbling at my breasts. I gripped the bed frame and quickened my movement. A thick purple vein bulged down the front of his head. Then his arms tightened and I smelled salt as his face turned pleasure-red.

The very second it was over I slid my fingers into the guy's pocket. His eyes sprang open, his ecstasy broken. He took hold of my wrist.

'Tomorrow!' he snapped.

'Fuck you.'

He slapped me dopily around the face.

'Tomorrow – or not at all.'

I slumped my shoulders and climbed off him.

'OK. Tomorrow,' I said.

I hung my head and reached for my shoes. My cheek was hurting.

He yawned: 'Good girl.' Then he closed his eyes, patted the letter and lolloped back on to the bed.

I looked at him then. I could see right up his nostrils. He had a wart just inside one of them. It was sprouting hair. I took one of my shoes. I stood over him. With all my strength I struck him in the face with the heel. He screamed very loud. He put his hands to his eye. I struck him in the face again. This time he let out a roar. I pulled at his jacket and grabbed the letter. I wobbled back; he lurched up. I threw the letter on to the floor. He took hold of my hair and he yanked down hard. He knocked the shoe out of my hand. He slapped me around the face over and over. His long nails scratched my cheek. Then he pushed me against the wall and clamped his hands around my throat and he roared and he squeezed, shaking my head. He was pressing down so hard I think he would have stopped me breathing if Abdesalam hadn't turned up. Suddenly he was there in the doorway in his cravat and apron. The mamba clutched at his pants and jumped from the bed. I gulped in air. I leapt down on the floor and snatched the letter. The two guys began to shout. Abdesalam threw his hands in the air in indignation. The mamba man stormed out. Before he did he turned to curse me. Small, square, bloody marks covered his cheeks and chin.

'You are wicked,' he spat, shaking his fists. 'You have much to fear!'

Once he had gone I began dressing. Abdesalam turned to me as I slipped on my shoes. His eyes were full of sadness. He touched the rim of his glasses.

'You are a prostitute?' he asked.

'Yeah, I guess so.'

I looked around for my coat.

'You have sold your body in my establishment?'

'In a way. It was the letter. He had my letter. He must have taken it from you!'

'Please pay me what you owe me and then leave here,' he said quietly. 'I am sorry. You cannot stay.'

Jula's letter to me was short. It was written on a postcard. It had a picture of mountains on it. Mountains and blue sky.

Marlena, I have left Sicily. I am in Como – just past Milan. I am staying in a pensione. *It's a real dump. It belongs to my mother's sister. I'm useless here. There's nothing to do. I don't know when I will leave. I don't know what I'm doing. Come if you can. Come soon. J*

I took the envelope and looked at the stamp. I checked the postmark – it was weeks old. There was no number on the card. Just the address and the name of the place. I gathered up my money. I didn't have what I owed in rent. I had no time to waste. Abdesalam would have to go without. Scared he might return, I pushed a few clothes into the case. I went over to the window and threw the case on to the heap of rubbish bags outside. I climbed out on to the sill, squatting on the ridge. It was wet and slippery. I clutched the drainpipe; it made a cracking sound. I fell and landed on the garbage pile. Then I picked myself up and I took my case and I crept back along the dock road. For the last time slinking under the bridge. I stopped for no one.

FOUR

I

The first thing I buy with Gianni Clari's money is a beret in turquoise mohair. Spring is coming – but I am ill-clothed for the north. I am at the edge of the Alps here. Como is cold. The man standing behind the stall at the railway station market holds a mirror to my face as I pull on the blue hat. He brings out a pair of gloves and drapes a scarf around my neck.

'*È bellissima!*' he cries, like he has just performed a miracle.

He smiles as I purchase the set.

I put my case into a lock-up. For the required four-digit code I choose the year that I was born. 1-9-7-4: I click the numbers into place and take a ticket from the slot. I am hungry again; I walk into the station bar. I buy slices of hot pizza. I wolf down fresh *tartine*. I buy cigarettes and order vodka. I talk to an old man who is smoking at the till. He is short and red-faced; burst blood vessels cover his nose. He has bright blue eyes. His hair is nicotine white. He shakes my hand; excited, he tells me his name. His breath smells of yesterday's drink as he shouts out: '*Sono Federico Barbarossa!*'

He chuckles at the irony. My hand is still clasped in his. In English his name means Red Beard. He tells me that when he was a young man he had red hair.

'Like my father and grandfather! As red as Siena brick!'

His face shakes and his eyes water as he asks me:

'And you, *signorina*? And you?'

I tell him I am visiting.

'Yes, you are in the mountain town!'

He slaps me on the back, taking a long look at me.

'Strangers are welcome here!'

I climb down from my stool to leave.

'Thank you,' I say.

I ask him if he knows the *Pensione Jessamine*. His face gleams with delight. He comes outside the bar with me and he points to the north – to where the mountains begin.

'I know everywhere in this town!'

I move nearer to him; I smell his age. I look faithfully along his pointing arm. His finger hovers above a sandstone spire in the middle distance.

'You see the church? *Vedi? Vedi?* The *Jessamine* is on Via Noto, the same!'

I turn to him; he shakes my hand again.

'At the other end of the street. You'll find it.'

It takes me almost an hour to reach Via Noto. I walk through the town centre and up into the suburbs, all the time keeping my eye on the church. When I get close I see it is boarded up. All its windows are smashed. The bell is locked. I am nervous now; my belly turns with anticipation. I go into the cemetery to smoke. I walk around to the back of the chapel and sit down on one of the tombs. Empty bottles lie in the grass. The vestry door is covered in graffiti. Someone has written in big red letters across the chipboard:

CHE SIAMO SENZA LA FIDUCIA? What are we without belief?

On Via Noto most of the houses look the same. They have flower balconies and built-in garages and huge wrought-iron gates. The *Pensione Jessamine* is different. It has no gate. Its sign is covered in dirt. I step on to the drive; the path to the door is buried in a mush of litter and wet leaves. I pull on the bell. A woman answers, poking her head out of a dark hall.

'*Non è qui*,' she tells me when I give her Jula's name.

He is not here. She tries to close the door. In protest I place my hand firm on the panel glass. I look the woman in the face as I push. She is just like Giosetta. She is maybe in her early sixties. She has long, greasy grey hair. She pushes back from the other side. She is wearing a little nightdress. Her nails are painted pink; her legs are bruised and purple-veined. As I stand there facing her I realize she is drunk.

'He isn't here any more, *signorina*,' she garbles. 'How many times do I need to say?'

'Then where?'

'How would I know?'

'You must know something.'

'Something. Ha, ha! Yes.'

She stumbles and leans on the door frame, revealing: 'He went to Milano. He got himself a job.'

'Where?' I demand. 'Doing what?'

'Don't ask me. I won't tell you. What are you, his lost little dog? Ha, ha! Get yourself another man. Jula is not here. You're out of luck.'

She pushes hard on the door with both her hands now. Blood pounds in my face and chest. My arms tense and shudder as I push back. She shouts upstairs, screaming 'Santo! Santo!' until a younger man comes running down. He is brown-skinned and wrapped in a bath towel. He looks like a TV hero as he rushes to shove his body weight against the wood. But as he does he starts; he weakens, deliberate. He looks like he wants to say something. He

247

looks at me like he knows me. His eyes turn soft. He lets me win for a moment. He lets me use the last of my strength. From the dark of the hall the woman opens her mouth and squawks: 'What are you waiting for?'

So he sighs and shoves, reluctant – and finally my arms buckle. The *pensione* door slams shut. I stand helpless on the steps. He knew me. I pull again and again on the bell. I bang with my fists. I get down on my knees. I flip open the letterbox; I put my mouth to it and plead:

'You must know where he is – please!'

No reply comes.

'I have no money! I have nothing! At least tell me where I can find work!'

'With no dignity? No manners?'

'I am desperate, *Signora*! I can't look any more.'

'Then give up, *carina*. Let him be.'

She comes to the box and draws a curtain across it. I let it snap shut and I sit on the steps – in the mush of the leaves, my head on the door. I can't face getting up. I can't face leaving. I sit there and close my eyes. I open them only when the door moves sudden. My body jolts forward. It is the man. He puts a finger to his lips. He squats down next to me in his towel and whispers:

'If you want work, try *La Sirena*. You're a club girl, right?'

He isn't Italian. He is Spanish or maybe South American. He smells clean. I nod my head.

'You're Marlena, aren't you? Jula was waiting for you. Like I said, try *La Sirena*. He used to go there a lot. It was his thing.'

2

Once a junkie always a junkie: that thing Analisa used to say. I don't know if I ever believed it. I mean, if I thought it could be so clear. She used to call it her sickness. Then I would tell her: 'Ana, you're not sick.'

'What am I then? What would you call me?'

'Not anything. Not sick. I don't know.'

I never asked her how it began. People always ask junkies that. Like there's got to be some great big reason. Like you can point back at it and call it the start. Besides, I pretty much knew what Analisa would say.

'Because I felt like it. Because it was there. Because I wanted to, Marlena. Why not?'

I have this high-rise memory. I am seventeen years old. It is a winter afternoon in England and I am knocking with black-gloved hands on the door of a top floor flat. It opens a crack; I know the guy behind it. He knows me too; he nods at me dull-eyed from under his hood. He is one of a group of guys who hang out here. Like all of them, he is older than me. I don't say anything to him; I smile. I walk past him down a dark hall to the room where the others will be. He slides a bolt across the door and follows me.

There is no electric in the flat; the room is cold and lit with shafts of sun. The guys are hunched on the floor around a table with their coats on – all quiet, somehow;

all looking in. Their mood is new to me. Usually they are ranting; drinking cans and smoking weed, maybe snorting a bit of speed. But like I said, no one is talking. And there's this smell in the air, like vinegar, like metal.

'What's going on?' I say, as I take my gloves off.

The guys don't answer. They keep on crouching at the table. And this smell, this metal smell, it gets right in my head. I walk to the group; they make a space for me. One of them holds a small foil tube. He is nervous; he sits clicking his jaw and twitching. He is waiting for something. He is waiting for his turn. And this other guy, Suggy – well, Suggy has a lighter held in one hand and a foil square in the other. The square has something on it, some dark powder. Suggy holds it very careful between his finger and thumb. And he asks the guy with the twitch and the tube: 'Ready to go?'

The tube guys nods. Suggy holds the foil square over the lighter flame. And the stuff on it is smoking and moving – and the smell becomes very strong. And it's bubbling up in balls and running in a little hot brown river – and the tube guy is ducking his head up and down now over the smoke. He is sucking through the tube and the others are watching him like he is important – and I don't know why but I watch him like he is important too. Then he finishes. All the smoke is gone. I feel his arm suddenly at my shoulder. He is handing me the tube. And he says to me, Follow the brown, chase it; he tells me this will be good. And he looks so placated. His twitch has gone. So I put the tube to my lips and follow the balls; I try to suck in their smoke – and as he burns up the junk Suggy adds: 'Oh yeah, Marlena. This is the big one. You're going to feel like a king.'

*

The snow on the mountain slopes that ring the border town of Como loses its whiteness when the sun drops. It turns the colour of the sky. As I leave there, evening is falling; all the peaks are brooding blue. I find the main road out and hitch a ride with a salesman. He drops me at a service station ten kilometres north of Milan.

'The club's behind there,' he tells me as I get out.

He buzzes down his electric windows to point past a Pizza Hut.

'What you want to work there for anyway? You want a job selling toothpaste?'

I laugh and shake my head.

'No.'

He grins all porcelain white and reaches on to his back seat. He thrusts a gift into my hand. Three silver-blue tubes of his latest product: *Perfect Smile*.

La Sirena sauna and gentlemen's club is run by a couple of Armenian guys. They are brothers. They don't speak much Italian. They have given the club a beach theme. All the blacked-out windows have mermaids painted on them. In the private rooms there are deckchairs. There is a palm tree on the main sign. It is full of Armenian and Latvian girls. I am much older than most of them. The brothers make a big deal of that. They tell me I am old meat. Still, they take me upstairs and on to a balcony. We pass the private rooms where the girls come in and out. We go into an office at the balcony end. It has a TV screen on the wall showing football and a glass front looking down on to the floor of the club. One of the brothers drops the window blinds. He makes me walk around. He tells me to take my shirt and trousers off.

'Thow what you do,' he lisps.

He folds his arms and sticks his chin out. He has black

hair down to his shoulders. His brother has a shaved head.
I kneel for them and I wiggle. I dance and I suck. I do
everything I have to until at last they agree to take me on.

'OK, OK,' says the skinhead. 'But no talking to the
babies, alright?'

He raises his hand in a warning. Then he explains the
deal. It isn't a good one. All the girls they have live in an
attic flat upstairs. My first three tricks on any night, they
tell me, will pay for my right to be here. My space sleeping
on a bare attic floor.

'And we take theventy five per thent of retht you earn,'
adds the lisper, handing me a bag of trashy clothes and old
shoes to look through. 'Thtarting tonight.'

The only girl my age in the club is a woman from Riga.
Her name is Lina. She has been working there a couple of
years. She speaks better Italian than the others. She speaks
some English too. After my first shift I drink gin with her
out the back. She tells me how she got here. She thought
she was coming to Italy to find a summer job. She was
coming to sell hot dogs, was what she thought. Then some
Latvian guys met her at Milan airport and made her suck
their dicks in the back of their van. There was no hot dog
job. They laughed at that and beat her up. They took her
passport, told her they'd kill her if she tried to run. They
cut her face and made her fuck them, one after the other.
Then they took her north in the middle of the night and
sold her to the club.

Lina has pipe blisters on her lips. She has green eyes and
pocked skin and her fringe cut very short. Scars cover her
arms and hands. She is skeleton thin. She takes me upstairs
and she shows me the attic. It has two rooms, both with
garret windows. It is full of skinny Latvian girls dressing
and sleeping on the floors. There is a fridge and a broken
sofa, a sink with a shower-head fitted on to the cold tap. I

sit down on the floor next to Lina as she cleans the paint off her nails.

'What are you doing here anyway?' she asks. 'You're Italian – you could work better places.'

'I'm looking for a guy. He comes in here.'

She wipes the make-up from her eyes. It smears over the pocks of her cheeks. When she has finished I take out my photograph of Jula and I put it in her hands.

'The gypsy?' she says.

'Yeah.'

'I know him. He comes in regular. I haven't seen him in a while though. Strange guy.'

She stands up and removes her vest. Her breasts are slack. They seem to stare at me. I swallow hard.

'Does he go with anyone?'

'Sometimes.'

She pulls off her skirt, her shoes and her pants. She stands in front of me naked.

'Yeah, he does. He usually goes with me.'

She walks away from me and stands at the sink; I stare at her ravaged body.

'He's not interested in the kids. He's a five-minute job!' she shouts, rubbing soap between her legs.

'How come you know him?' she asks. 'Is he your guy?'

I don't answer her. I watch her. I watch her wash. She shivers at the basin. Her skin turns red and blotchy. She pulls a towel across her back and bends over, drying herself down.

'He doesn't come in so much now. Must have got himself another girlfriend. Want me to tell him you're here when he comes in again?'

'Yeah.'

She walks towards me. She has baby marks on her belly. Her nipples stick out like bulletheads. She sits with her legs open on the floor. She rummages in a plastic bag and puts on a T-shirt. She takes out a pair of socks and shakes them. A wrap of gear falls out. She puts the socks on, then a pair of old jeans. She brings out a lighter, a filter, a spoon. She takes the spoon to the sink and drips water into it. I think about her body. Her bullet nipples. Her baby scars. I think about Jula on top of her, moving and moaning and coming inside her in a flash. I'd like to take her into one of the private rooms. I'd like to slap her. I'd like to kick her and scratch her and fuck her with my hand.

'Hey Marlena, what's up? You look a little pale. You do this shit? You want shot?'

She takes out a set of works from her carrier bag. I can't talk. Suddenly everything about Lina makes me want to scream and cry. Her body, her voice, the way she moves as she hands me one of her stockings to tie round my arm. The way she whispers to me in marred English as I bring up a vein: 'Sure you want shot. Sure.'

3

It is mid-August, the night of *ferragosto*, when Jula returns to *La Sirena*. It is almost a year since I have seen him. I recognize him at once. I am standing up on the balcony; I have just finished a job. I look down over the rail and on to the club floor and I see him walk through the big black doors. He is wearing a suit. His hair is cropped short. He is clean-shaven. He is thin.

I watch him sit down alone in a booth. A couple of Latvian girls saunter over, trying to get his attention. I see Lina push past them and serve him a drink. Jula greets her with the bones of a smile. He takes off his coat. He puts his arm around her waist. Lina sits on his knee and strokes his head. Then she whispers in his ear and they both start scanning the club. They are looking for me; I know that. When Lina spots me she shouts my name. Jula looks up sharp. He looks up and sees me standing there above him – tall, in black bikini pants and heels, my face made-up like he has never seen it, my breasts and belly greased and bare. His mouth opens, wordless, as I stay still, staring down. He hands Lina some money. She refuses it, shaking her head. So he leaves it on the table; he walks across the room and up the metal stairs – and then he is standing with me, Jula Schigghiapeddi, Jula of The Little Meat Squeals, leaning with me on the balcony rail. He is different now. He has one of those Berghaus coats – a red one, slung over his shoulder. He wears leather shoes. He smells of cologne. I don't know what to do. I kiss him hello – in the Italian way.

'*Ciao*, Jula,' I say.

I press my cheeks to his. His skin flushes. Our lips don't touch. I take him into the room I have been working in. We sit down on the bed.

'You're here,' I utter, studying his face.

Grey shadows have reached his eyes.

'I'm here.'

'I went to Como,' I ramble, 'but I was too late. That guy there, that friend of your aunt. He told me sometimes you visit the club.'

'Santo.'

'Yeah, Santo. He said – he said the farm got sold.'

Jula sighs and puts his head in his hands.

'The farm got sold, Franco got pulled in. Everything went to shit.'

'Where's Lola?'

'With my mother in Catania. I'm going to try and bring her here Marlena, when I can get it together. She's all right there. *Mamma* bought a restaurant. She's got this friend who's going to help her. She says she's making a new start.'

'And Savio?'

Jula smiles shakily. I have to fight the urge to throw up.

'He's dead.'

We sit without speaking, the past rolling through my head. Downstairs the club throbs, then Jula says: 'It was Alex who did it. Remember – from the caravan? He wanted to do it! He just raged up to the farm, he didn't have a plan. He said he didn't care what happened. He went and found Savio down in the *cantina* and shot him in the back and the leg. He died in the hospital. Alex was charged. Franco too. Alex got a short sentence because of the

Anželika thing. I think I saw your friend Dana by the way. Franco managed to get out on bail.

I touch Jula's suit collar, his shirt lapel, his tie.

'You're earning money,' I say.

He laughs.

'I'm a *valido* draughtsman.'

'You made it?'

'Not really, Marlena, no.'

He touches the back of his neck in a way that means he is nervous. I wait for him to explain.

'I'm fucking the boss's daughter,' he says eventually. 'I'm living in her flat.'

He lights a cigarette. He offers me one.

'I'm a whore!' he says. 'I know.'

'I had to fuck both the bosses to get in this place,' I tell him.

'Jesus Christ.'

We laugh. He looks my body over.

'You've recovered all right?'

'Just about.'

'You've lost weight.'

He pauses. Then he asks me: 'You back on the gear?'

I face him. 'Can you tell? Now and then. I can't believe you're a rich guy,' I say.

He smiles; his black eyes stay fixed on me. He says: 'Listen, you want to go somewhere else? Into the city? We could get something to eat. I mean you're probably not hungry. You junkies never eat! Ana was always half-starved. Still. You want to come?'

'Sure,' I tell him.

'You going to manage without a fix? How much you doing anyway?'

His questions quiet and intimate.

'Just a bag a day. Not much.'

'I can probably get you some Valium.'

Jula of The Little Hurts.

'Come on,' he adds. 'I think I know where we can score in Milan.'

At the petrol place down from *La Sirena*, Jula calls a taxi. It comes and picks us up by the pumps. It speeds us into Milan. From inside the car the city looks grand, unreal; we pass statues and lit fountains; we drive down streets all lined with flags.

'Here for the parades?' the driver asks.

Jula tells him yes. We climb out at the *duomo*; we hear carnival music. Jula reaches into his wallet and tips him well.

Once we have got some sleepers we go looking for a pizzeria. The one we choose to eat in is busy and loud. Bad caricatures of film stars line the walls. I peer at them, trying to work out who they are. I laugh at the bad Humphrey Bogart, the Marilyn Monroe. With Jula there suddenly everything is funny; I am giddy, clumsy. I smash a glass. Jula reaches over and squeezes my knee as a waiter appears and sweeps up the mess. A woman near us makes a face like an owl.

'*Che faccia da gufo!*' Jula jokes to me, under his breath.

He is going to order *calzone*, he says. I have no appetite. I pick ice cream and chocolate sauce. When the food arrives I watch Jula eat. He puts his elbows up on the table. I put mine up too. He grins, his mouth full of food. We drink thin red wine. We smoke cigarettes. We finish a pack. We buy another from a machine. Then we go to a club where Jula buys me heroin.

While I wait I drink tequilas in a long silver room. We buy more cigarettes. We watch young Milan men dancing in blue neon light. We dance too. We laugh at ourselves. We leave the club.

It is past midnight when we begin walking the streets. We are searching for a hotel. The parades are beginning. Fireworks crack in the sky. The streets are jammed; we get caught in a procession. We move with the crowds for a while in the sound of drums. Young men hurry down the sides of the streets carrying casks of wine on their backs. Women wearing feather-masks clap their hands. There are trumpets and clarinets, kids hanging down from first-floor windows, yelling: '*Buon Ferragosto! Buona Festa!*'

They delve into boxes and begin scattering paper petals in the air. Jula returns their good wishes as he walks with me. It starts to rain. He points to the green and white awning of a big hotel. We leave the parade.

'*Buon Ferragosto!*' he shouts up to the kids. '*Ciao ragazzi!*'

Petals fall on our shoulders, sticking to our damp hair.

In the mirrors of the main lift at the Hotel David, Jula and I look like newlyweds. We are wet, bedraggled; we are covered in paper flowers. We stare at our reflections. We do not brush the petals off. A porter stands at the lift with us; he faces the door. He wears a tartan waistcoat. When he ushers us out at the mezzanine he calls me *Signora*. He walks ahead of us, whistling, brisk. We pass door after door; I count each one. At every threshold I will the porter to stop. As if he can read the thought in my head, Jula speaks the numbers out loud. Two thousand and thirty. Two thousand and thirty one. He takes my hand.

At door 2094 the porter swings round to face us.

'We have arrived!' he announces.

He takes a key from his pocket and thrusts it happily into the lock. He pushes the door open and steps into the room. We follow him in; he turns on a bright light and half-sings: 'You have air-conditioning, radio and Sky TV!'

He flashes the breakfast menu in front of our faces and demonstrates the phone. He reaches into drawers and pulls out items. An iron, a hairdryer, a bible painted with gold leaf. We stand together and we watch as he darts around in his waistcoat, ensuring we have coffee and towels and new soap, showing us this and that. When he finally leaves with a little bow, we hang our coats up and we face each other. Jula reaches to the wall and turns off the light. We kiss now with our mouths; we undress in the sudden dark. We climb into the cold, clean bed. We hear laughter on the street below. I pull myself on top of Jula. He weeps, feels out my scars.

About the Author

Photo: James Barr

RACHEL INGRAMS was born in 1974. *Blood Tender* is her first novel and is drawn in part from the times when she lived and worked in Sicily, aged nineteen, and when she lived in a gypsy tenement in Prague, aged twenty-four. Rachel now lives in Sheffield where she works with young people around their drug and alcohol use.

Acknowledgements

Acknowledgements

I'd like to express my heartfelt thanks to Manjusvara and Ananda for their unfailing belief in my work right from the start, and to Dhivan and Tone for their generosity and time; to Emma, Alan and Luke at Tindal Street, who always seemed to know where I was trying to go; to James, for enduring and photographing the real me; to Cathy, Annie and Beth for their enthusiasm and friendship and the nights we stayed up thinking; to Rosie, whose love is a daily reason to create – and of course to the real Black-Eyed Man, who kept the fire of *Blood Tender* burning long after the original spark.